K
/05

The Rupa Book of
Indian Love Stories

The Rupa Book of
Indian Love Stories

C. A. Kincaid

Introduction by
Ruskin Bond

Rupa & Co

Typeset copyright © Rupa & Co 2003
Introduction copyright © Ruskin Bond 2003

First published 2003
Second impression 2003

Published by
Rupa & Co

7/16, Ansari Road, Daryaganj,
New Delhi 110 002

Sales Centres:

Allahabad Bangalore Chandigarh Chennai
Hyderabad Jaipur Kathmandu Kolkata
Ludhiana Mumbai Pune

Typeset in 11 pts. ClassicalGaramond by
Nikita Overseas Pvt Ltd
1410 Chiranjiv Tower
43 Nehru Place
New Delhi 110 019

Printed in India by
Rekha Printers Pvt Ltd
A-102/1 Okhla Industrial Area, Phase-II
New Delhi 110 020

Contents

Introduction

*D*uring my adventures among old books, I have always kept a keen look-out for anything by Charles A. Kincaid, C.V.O., I.C.S., (Retd.), to give him his full by-line. Good secondhand bookshops are becoming as rare as the books they once offered, but if an intrepid book-hunter keeps searching he may still turn up a treasure or two. Such as Kincaid's *Tales of Old Ind*, rediscovered and now presented to the discriminating reader under the title *The Rupa Book of Indian Love Stories*; for that in effect is what they are: fourteen legendary romances from Punjab, Haryana, Sind, Kathiawar and Rajasthan. The loves of Suhni and Mehar, Hir and Ranjho, Umar and Marai, Momul and Rano, and other star-crossed lovers are beautifully captured in Kincaid's charming retellings.

Who was Kincaid? At this point in time it is difficult to discover much about his personal life, and seventy or more years ago writers did not project themselves through the media as eagerly as they do now. They preferred to stay in the background, allowing their work to do the talking. But we do know that Kincaid was a British Civil Servant who lived in India for the greater part of his life, serving in Kathiawar, Gujarat, Maharashtra, the Sind of undivided India, and elsewhere. Along the way he picked up a great deal of information on a large variety of subjects, and upon his retirement he took to writing, turning out works that were both informative and entertaining. A short list of some of his titles will give you some idea of his versatility:

Sri Krishna of Dwarka
Deccan Nursery Tales
Tales from the Indian Epics
A History of the Maratha People
Tales of Pandharpur
A Tale of the Tulsi Plant
The Land of Ranji and Duleep
The Rani of Jhansi and other essays
Indian Christmas Stories
Heroines of India
Our Parsi Friends
Indian Lions

And many more!

Kincaid took a lively interest in all aspects of Indian life, its cultural diversity, religion, folklore, history, customs. I was able to include three of his excellent ghost stories in *Ghost Stories from the Raj*, a macabre shikar story in *The Rupa Book of Great Animal Stories*, and his re-creation of Alexander's Indian Campaign in *The Rupa Book of True Tales of Mystery and Adventure*. He was particularly fond of the Kathiawar States, referring to them as "the land of Ranji and Duleep", those legendary cricketers who played for England long before an Indian national team came into being. Many of Kincaid's books deserve reprinting, and this volume is a start in that direction.

Ruskin Bond
April, 2003

Punho and Saswi

Once upon a time when king Dilu Ra was king in Sind he named as one of his governors a rich Brahman called Naun. The Brahman had vast wealth and great stores of jewels but he had neither son nor daughter. Although he spent thousands of rupees on yogis and anchorites, still he and his wife remained childless and unhappy. One day, his wife came to hear of an old astrologer, who was versed not only in the wisdom of India but in that of Greece also. She said to her husband, "Life without children is like a starless night; let us journey and consult this astrologer, for, so they say, he is wise above all men." Naun after some hesitation consented, and with a great store of gold he and his wife set out for the sage's hermitage.

When the sage saw the Brahman and his wife coming, he rose and greeted them courteously and led them to his hut. There he asked them what they needed. The Brahman fell at his feet with folded hands and cried, "Reverend Sir, pray for us to the Almighty that He bestow upon us a child, for our lives are lonely and bitter without one." The sage thought for a moment, took his dice box and cast the dice. After noting the numbers, he brought out his "ramal" or magic mirror. He looked into it and said, "I can see Jupiter close to Mars. The Almighty will vouchsafe to you a daughter, but she is fated to wed a Musulman husband." Tears came into the eyes of the old Brahman and he begged the sage to alter his daughter's fate; but the astrologer, although he pitied his guest, could do nothing for him. "What God has written, He has written," he murmured and dismissed him. In due course the Brahman's wife bore her lord a child. He asked the midwife its sex, for he had always hoped against hope that it might be a son and so prove the astrologer wrong. "The baby is a girl," replied the midwife. The Brahman's heart sank within him, for he saw that the sage's prophecy was coming true. "I shall not keep the accursed brat in my house," he said angrily: "bring me a stone that I may batter it to pieces, or else let me throw it into the fire." The Brahman's wife agreed that they should get rid of the child, but she would not consent to its death. "Put it in a box," she said, "and let it float down the Indus. Someone may see the child and care for it." The Brahman got a box and inside it he put the sleeping baby. He put by the baby a bag of gold and jewels, and padlocked the lid. Then he carried the box to the river-bank and flung it into the water. The current caught it and took it bobbing and tossing down stream until it reached Bhambhora town. There a washerman, Mahomed by name, saw it as it floated by near the bank. He waded into the water, pulled the box ashore, forced open the lock and inside saw a lovely little baby girl. He lifted her out and then saw the bag of gold and jewels. His eyes dancing with joy, he took his double treasure home. His wife who had no children was overjoyed and she and her husband adopted the foundling as their own. They called their neighbours, friends, and castemen to see the baby girl. Then they gave her the name of Saswi. As the years passed, the beautiful babe grew into a still more beautiful girl and men would neglect their business and hang about the lanes near the washerman's house, just to catch a glimpse of her lovely face. With the bag of gold and jewels found in the box, the washerman bought the girl finery and ornaments and a two-storeyed house with a rose-garden round it. There, Saswi would call her girl friends and with them pass the hours weaving or walking among the rose-beds near her home.

Now at this time there lived a famous Baluch warrior named Jam Ari. So many were his victories and so great his valour, that his fellow-tribesmen hailed him as their leader and placed on his head the turban of all Kech and Kohistan. He had five sons, Chuno, Punho, Hoto, Nakro and Noto. All were brave, handsome men, but by far the bravest and handsomest was the second son, Punho. Far and wide the Baluch chief levied dues from the caravans; far and wide too, his sons raided the lands of those who defied him. Unhappily the fame of Saswi's beauty had reached this distant land and haunted Punho's thoughts. One day a merchant, by name Babyo, came to Kohistan. Jam Ari greeted him cordially and was so pleased with his address and bearing that he remitted the customs due on his goods. In a few days Babyo had sold all the goods that he had brought and had bought others to sell elsewhere. He begged leave to go, saying that he wished to sell his new wares in Bhambhora. Jam Ari reluctantly gave him leave to go. But when he said good-bye to Punho, the young prince whispered in his ear, "Seek Saswi at Bhambhora and send me a secret message to tell me whether she is as beautiful as men say."

The merchant smiled assent and went towards his camels. The camel-men tightened the girths, jerked the nose-strings and the caravan started. In front with stately step walked the seasoned black-headed camels. Behind them went the young camels. In this manner the caravan travelled day after day until they reached Bhambhora. There, Babyo took a lodging and displayed his goods, until the fame of his merchandise and of his beautiful face—for he was very handsome—spread all over the town; and young and old, men and women, flocked to his lodging. A day or two later, Babyo went by the house where Saswi lived. She and her girl-companions were playing together, when she chanced to see from her upper window Babyo passing in the street below. Struck by his handsome face, she begged her girl-friend Saki to ask the merchant to come upstairs. Saki ran into the street and gave Babyo Saswi's message. He smiled and taking with him some precious wares went with Saki into Saswi's house. As he was showing his goods to Saswi, she whispered into his ear, "Listen, Sir Merchant, you have caught my heart as with a hook, and I cannot help but love you." Babyo did not at first reply but looked at Saswi, fascinated by her beauty. Then he thought to himself, "Washer-girl though she be, she is worthy of Punho. Her face is like the moon and in her form I can see no fault. Her beauty makes her a fitting bride even for a prince." Then he shook his head at Saswi and said, "Nay, hear me, fair maiden, do not waste your thoughts on me. I know one, Punho by name, far more worthy of you than I am. I am only a common man. But to him all Kech and Kohistan pay homage. I am but a trader. He is a prince and open-handed and generous. No beggar is ever in want when he is by. He has horses and camels and stores a gold and silver, and soldiers and door-keepers and clerks. Indeed, I too am in his service. I have not spoken of his beauty, for it is beyond my words to describe. Wait until you see him and them only can you judge how fair he is. May God grant that you meet him some day."

Saswi's thoughts turned from Babyo to the prince, and she longed to see him of whom the merchant spoke in such glowing words. "God grant," she echoed, "that some day I may see Prince Punho." Then, turning to Babyo, she cried, "Go, Sir Merchant, go and bring him here, this beautiful youth, for I long to see him!" Babyo took leave of the lovely girl, and, going home, sent for a letter-writer. When the letter-writer came, he bade him write two letters. The first ran, "I have seen Saswi. She is but a washerman's daughter, but God has given her perfect beauty. Her face rivals the moon in beauty and the sun in brightness. Come with all speed in a merchant's dress, and bring with you a load of attar and ambergris." The second letter ran, "Come in haste to help me. The men of Bhambhora have cruelly seized and imprisoned me, saying that I owe them custom dues. Come, Prince Punho, for only you can save me." These two letters he gave to a messenger, who on a swift camel soon reached Punho's country. To Punho the messenger explained that the first letter was for Punho alone, the second for Punho's father. The prince read the first letter and his eyes shone when he read of Saswi's beauty. Then he took the second letter to Jam Ari, who had it read to him. The king grew angry when he heard that his friend, the merchant Babyo, had been treated wrongfully. "Go, Punho," he cried, "go; kill his enemies and free him."

Punho bade the messenger go back to Bhambhora and tell Babyo that he would come with all speed. He then took a store of ambergris and attar, and packing it in boxes, fastened them secretly on his camel. His camel-saddles and saddle-cloths were bright with gold and silver; and bead-necklaces and strings of bells hung round the camels' necks. The prince and his men donned their embroidered coats, wound round their heads mighty turbans, fastened round their waists their green trousers and flung over their shoulders white scarfs heavy with gold and silver lace. When Punho's party was ready, Jam Ari came bringing with him Punho's brother Chuno. "Take him with you," said the king, "you may need him, and he will always keep his shoes by him that he may be ready to serve you. But come back as soon as you can, for you, Punho, are my favourite son. Come back in triumph with drums playing in front of you." Punho bade his father and mother good-bye and he and his men started. The king and queen went home to weep, but Punho and his men played and sang together to beguile the journey, until the whole Heaven was gay with their music and the tinkling of the camel's bells. As night fell, the caravan reached Kahir Bela. There they camped for the night and next morning all the village came to see the travellers. Now in Kahir Bela there lived a lovely sonar† girl named Sahjan. When she saw Punho's face, she felt that she would love him and him only all her life. She sent an old woman and begged him to show her his goods. "I will take all your attar and ambergris and give you instead diamonds and pearls and rubies." So ran the message, for by it she hoped to tempt Punho to visit her. Punho went back with the old woman, but he would not sell his goods. "I need them," he said, "at Bhambhora." But he willingly stayed the night with Sahjan. She prepared for him a splendid meal of which he ate most heartily. Next day, however, in spite of her tears and entreaties, he joined his men, and once again the air was filled with the noise of their singing and the music of their bells as they rode from Kahir Bela; nor did they halt again until they reached Bhambhora.

As they came close to the town, Punho sent for Babyo, who pointed out to him a camping-ground south of the city. There,

---

† Sonar is the goldsmith caste.

the two princes made the camel-men unload their camels, pitch the tents, spread the carpets and in all ways prepare a camp. They got out their musk and ambergris and attar, and displayed them as if they were a party of merchants. The news spread that a great trader had come to Bhambhora and it soon came to Saswi's ear. "This must be prince Punho," she said to herself; "he has come here at Babyo's bidding." She called together her girl-companions and decked with jewels, they walked one following the other like demoiselle cranes flighting in the winter twilight. They were all about the same age, but the loveliest by far was Saswi. She had eyes like a deer, teeth like a row of pearls and a nose like a slice of ripe mango; her breasts rose like two pomegranates beneath her bodice, her hair was braided with gold, and she walked like a peahen in the early springtime. The jingling of the girl's anklets warned Punho's door-keepers that strangers were coming, and after taking the prince's leave they opened the tent-doors for the girls to enter. Inside the tents were spread all Punho's treasures, and the girls began eagerly to bargain for them and haggle about the price. But once Punho's and Saswi's eyes met, they had no thoughts for aught else than each other. And when the other girls had finished their bargaining and wished to return home, poor Saswi's heart was aflame with love for Punho. Nor was the prince less in love with Saswi. Sadly, Saswi left the tent to follow her companions; but when she reached her house she called Saki and said, "My eyes are full of tears, my heart is full of fire; bring Punho to me or I shall die."

Saki tried to soothe her but Saswi could not rest until Saki promised to see Saswi's parents next day and win their consent to her marriage with the strange merchant. Next day, Saki went to Saswi's mother and said, "Lady, a trader has come to Bhambhora from a far country. In beauty he rivals both the sun and moon.

Offer him your daughter in marriage, for a handsomer or richer husband you will never find." "But of what caste is he?" asked the washerwoman surprised. Just then Mahomed came and his wife told him what Saki had said. As they were talking together, Babyo walked past in the street below. "There goes the merchant's clerk," said Saki; "send for him and ask him what the merchant's caste is." Mahomed did so. Babyo guessing the cause of the question, answered, "He has often told me that he was at one time a washerman, but he had to flee from his country and so became a trader." Mahomed then begged Babyo to invite Punho to his house. Babyo did so. Punho gladly accepted the invitation. When he and Babyo came, Mahomed, to test the prince, said, "You are, so they tell me, a washerman by caste; pray help me to wash some clothes." Saying this, Mahomed gave the prince some soap and a bundle of silk clothes. Babyo had told the prince that he must declare himself a washerman by caste: so he took the clothes, although he had no idea how to wash them. As he was carrying them away his brother Chuno met him and said angrily, "Is it true what I hear? Are you going to disgrace us by marrying a washer-girl?" Punho answered him. "Brother, there is no disgrace in marrying where one loves." Leaving Chuno silent, he went to the river-bank. There, in his efforts to wash the clothes, he tore them into shreds. As he was looking sadly at the heap of rags, Saswi came up to him and cheered him with a smile. "Do not despair, my Prince," she said; "put a gold piece in the pocket of each dress and there will be no complaints." This Punho did, and taking the clothes back to their owners told them to look in the pockets. They did so, and as their fingers touched the gold their anger died within them. When Mahomed learnt that Punho had washed and returned the clothes and that none of the owners complained of the washing, he was satisfied that the merchant was really by caste a washerman. He agreed to the marriage and preparing a mighty feast he wedded together Punho and Saswi. But prince Chuno would take no part in the gaiety: with a heavy heart he returned with his men to Jam Ari's country and told how Punho had been snared by Saswi's beauty. The Jam's face grew black with grief and anger. Three days he spent in lamenting. Then he bade Chuno and Hoto and Noto ride forth and bring back Punho. The three princes rode to Bhambhora, and with soft words on their lips but with hearts full of guile, greeted Punho and Saswi as their brother and sister. Neither Punho nor his bride suspected evil. Chuno told them that Jam Ari had approved the marriage, and in their joy they feasted the princes right royally for several days. One night the princes put a drug in the wine that Punho and Saswi were drinking, and at midnight, when both were fast asleep, they tore Punho from Saswi's side and placing him helpless on a camel's back they rode away with all speed towards Kech. When Saswi woke next morning and found herself alone, her cries roused all the neighbours. She told them her story and vowed that she would follow Punho on foot, until she either found him or fell by the wayside. All tried to dissuade her except Saki, who approved her grief and bade her keep her vow.

Saswi set out on foot, following the track of the princes' camels, until as night fell and she was faint with walking, she came to a goat-herd's hut. Approaching it she asked the goat-herd if he had seen a caravan go by. But the goat-herd, as he looked at Saswi, was overcome by her beauty, and instead of answering her, seized her and tried to drag her inside his hut. Saswi first called to Punho for help but no answer came. Then she prayed aloud, "O! Merciful Allah! Open the earth beneath my feet and save me from this wretch!" As she prayed the earth suddenly opened and snatched Saswi from the goat-herd's grasp. Then it closed again, but the end of Saswi's sari remained sticking out of the ground. The goat-herd fled to his hut and hid himself in terror.

Now at noon Punho awoke from his drugged sleep and found himself lying on a camel's back. He asked Chuno how he came there. When his younger brother told him that at Jam Ari's order they were taking him back to Kech, the prince sprang from the camel to the ground. When Chuno and his brothers stopped their camels and tried to take him, he drew his sword so fiercely that they were afraid and left him. Distracted he made his way back towards Bhambhora until he came to the spot where Saswi had vanished. Close by he saw the goat-herd, who had got over his fright and was returning from his hut. The prince asked him whether he had seen a fair woman pass that way, for he felt sure that Saswi would try to follow him. The goat-herd told him that a woman but a short time before had come there and that suddenly the earth had swallowed her up. In proof of what he said, he pointed to the end of Saswi's sari sticking out of the ground. The prince at once recognised it. Then he prayed to Allah that the earth might swallow him also. Allah had pity on the unhappy youth. The earth opened at his feet. In the yawning pit he saw Sawi lying. Her voice called to him from the depths. He sprang into the chasm, and the earth, closing over their heads, joined in death the prince and the washer-girl.

King Dyach and Bijal

Once upon a time there lived in the Girnar Fort in Kathiawar a famous king called King Dyach. One day his sister went to an anchorite and asked him to obtain a son for her by his prayers. The anchorite prayed and then said, "Lady, you will have a son, but he will cause King Dyach to lose his head." "But," cried the princess, aghast at the anchorite's words, "I would sooner have no son than one who will kill my brother the king." The anchorite shook his head and answered: "What I have said, I have said." Less than a year—for how can an anchorite's words prove false?—the princess bore her husband a son. The princess, fearing for her brother, put the baby in a box and threw the box into the Indus, in the hope that a crocodile would swallow it. But no crocodile saw the box, and the great river bore the child safely to Ajmir where ruled a great king called Anira.

When the anchorite heard what the princess had done, he went to king Anira's country and pointed out the box to a

Charan† man and woman. The Charans dragged the box from the river and opened it. When the woman saw a beautiful baby-boy inside, she gave a cry of joy and taking him out adopted him as her own. "He is tiny now," she said, "but he will be big some day. Then he will repay us for our care and trouble." The husband agreed; they took the baby home and called him Bijal. When the little boy was six years old, they put him to graze their donkeys and horses. He drove them daily to the grazing-ground, and as he went, he sang and played on his Charan's fiddle so beautifully, that the deer stopped to listen to his music. One day Bijal came to a spot where some hunters had killed a deer. They had roasted and eaten the flesh, but before going away they had stretched the guts on two branches of a tree. Now the guts had this magic quality, that when the south wind blew, they gave forth such wondrous music that the antelope and the wild bear came near the tree, craning their necks to hear every note. When Bijal heard the music and learned whence it came, he took down the dead deer's guts and fastened them as strings to his fiddle. Then he drew his bow across them and began to play. The wild deer had stopped before to listen to his playing, but now the birds came out of the sky and perched on his shoulder; and the beasts of the forest crouched low at his feet, drawn to him by the witchery of his playing. Nor could they leave him so long as his music lasted. So, playing as he went, he drew them after him to the Charans' huts. There the Charans picked out what deer they wanted for food. Then Bijal stopped playing. At once the charm ceased and the birds flew back into the sky and the wild beasts raced back to their lairs in the plains or the woods. The Charans were overjoyed at the skill of their foster-son. "If we snared deer

---

† Charans are the hereditary bards of the Rajput chiefs.

once or twice a year," they said, "we thought ourselves fortunate. But the boy catches them whenever he wishes. He is indeed a gift worthy of the great river." The fame of Bijal's playing spread so, that the Charans without difficulty found for him a beautiful wife, with whom he lived happily for several years.

Now about the time that Bijal was born, one of king Anira's wives bore him a daughter. King Anira had already sixty daughters, but no son; so when his sixty-first daughter was born, he grew so angry that he put the baby-girl into a box and placing a bag of gold beside her put the box with its burden into the Indus. The Indus bore the baby-girl into a village which belonged to King Dyach. There a potter named Ratno saw the box and dragged it out of the water. He took out the little girl and carrying her home called her Surat. Now Ratno, although he lived in one of King Dyachs' villages, was a great favourite of King Anira and was always in attendance on him. One day Ratno obtained two months' leave from King Anira and went to his village. There the time passed so happily that before he knew it four months had gone by. Then he remembered that he had only been given two months' leave; you are going to your death." But Ratno answered: "Even if it is so, I must go. I have been guilty of one fault, let me not commit another." So, mounting his horse, he rode along the road to Ajmir.

Now King Anira was very angry when Ratno did not return to his court after two months. He said to his guards, "When Ratno comes to court, you must kill him directly after he has visited me." Thus, when Ratno reached King Anira's palace, he noticed that the guards saluted him no longer nor did they take his horse respectfully as they had been used to do. Ratno entered the palace and made his way into the king's presence. But the king scowled at him and turned his head away. Then Ratno said boldly, "O king, why do you thus turn your head away from me?" The king answered him angrily, "You promised to come back in two months and you have stayed away four." "Oh king!" said Ratno; "hear me before you condemn me." "Well, what have you to say?" growled the king. "O king, I have a daughter who is of an age to marry. I have been seeking a husband for her, but I have not yet succeeded." "Then why not marry her to me?" said the king. Ratno was so pleased that he at once consented, and he rode off on the king's riding-camel to fetch Surat, the girl whom he had picked out of the river Indus. In front of him rode a squadron of royal guards, who beat kettle-drums until the whole heavens resounded. When the party drew near to King Dyach's frontier, Ratno told Anira's guards to return. "If you ride like this," he said, "beating your drums, King Dyach will think that you have come to make war on him." So the guards turned back and Ratno rode on alone to his home and married Surat to King Anira by proxy. Afterwards he had a torchlight procession through the streets. Now King Dyach was sitting by the window of a palace in the great Girnar fort, and when he saw the torchlight procession, he sent a manservant to learn the cause of it. The man brought back the news that Ratno was marrying his daughter to King Anira. "Bring Ratno here," ordered King Dyach. The servant again went out and summoned Ratno. "Why did you not give your daughter to me?" asked the king. "I am a poor man," replied Ratno; "you are a king. I did not imagine you would accept her." The king thought for a moment; then he said, "Well, she shall be my wife now. I will settle with King Anira." With these words he sent his guards to seize Surat and bring her to the palace.

In course of time King Anira came to know that King Dyach had carried off Surat. He called together a mighty army and marched to the Girnar fort. But when he tried to storm the fort he failed, for his cannon could not reach the walls, they were so high above the plain: and after suffering great losses he retreated to Ajmir. But his heart still burned, with hatred against King Dyach; so he put his costliest jewels on a plate and gave the plate to a slave to take through his country proclaiming that the jewels would be his who would bring the head of King Dyach to Ajmir.

When the slave came to the Charan's village, Bijal was not in his house, and in his absence his wife took the plate of jewels from the slave. When Bijal came back and learned what his wife had done, he grew very angry. "Woman," he said, "why did you take the plate? You have forced me to go on a hopeless quest. Yet, if I do not go, King Anira's men will come and kill us all and plunder our village.

Having said this, Bijal took his fiddle, tied to it a string of white shells, and putting on white garments, set forth on foot to the Girnar. When he drew near to the great fortress, he prayed to Allah, "O Lord! grant this my prayer, that I may snare King Dyach with my music, even as near my own village I have often snared the deer!" Then he began to play so sweet a melody, that all the townspeople ran into the streets and offered him alms. But he would take nothing, and all through the night he played, while the townspeople sat by his side, for they never felt sleepy so long as Bijal drew his bow across the strings.

Next morning the news of this strange beggar reached the ears of King Dyach. That evening he sent a palki for Bijal and bade him come to his palace. All that night Bijal played, until King Dyach in gratitude offered him as a gift any village in his kingdom. But Bijal shook his head. When morning broke, he went and rested some hours under a tree outside the city. That evening again, King Dyach sent for him, for he was falling into the boy's snare, just as the deer had done when Bijal led them to be slaughtered helplessly in the Charan's village. All that night and for three nights afterwards King Dyach listened enraptured to the magic melodies, until at last he said, "Ask me any boon you wish, and I will give it to you." This was the answer for which Bijal had plotted, and he cried, "O! king, the boon for which I ask is your head." The king, caught in the boy's toils, struggled in vain to free himself. He offered Bijal his costly raiment, his palaces, his houses, his treasure and his dancing girls. But Bijal merely shook his head, and taking up his fiddle began again to play; and as he played, the king's heart sank within him, for he knew that he could never free himself from the charm of the music. Indeed, he had no longer power to send Bijal away. The boy stayed in the palace and every evening boldly entered the king's chamber and began unasked to play. At last the king said, "O! of what use, Bijal, would my head be to you? I should be ashamed to give you so sorry a gift. Take my wealth and go on your way rejoicing." But the boy shook his head and answered, "You bade me choose my boon and I have chosen it. You cannot now break your promise. After all, O king, what is life without honour? Keep your promise; and even though your life ends, your fame will live for ever. Break your promise; and even though your life endures a few years longer, your fame will die to-day." The king could find no answer, for the magic music had clouded his wits just as it had clouded the wits of the birds and the forest-beasts; and he listened helplessly, while Bijal stood beside him and wound round and round him more firmly the web of his sorcery.

At last King Dyach bade Queen Surat try to free him from the net of the Charan. She sent a palki for Bijal, and just as the king had done, she offered him rich clothes and jewels and elephants. But the boy would not yield: "The king," he said, "has given me his word. He is no king if he breaks it."

When Dyach learnt that Surat had failed to rid him of Bijal, he went to his mother, Queen Khatu, and said: "What shall I do? If I give him my head, I must leave you and my wives, my kingdom, and my glory. Yet if I do not, he taunts me with breaking my word and he vows that all the world shall know my infamy." Queen Khatu replied, "My son, what is life? It is but a little thing, for no man knows how long his life lasts. You should not have made a rash promise, but now that you have made it, you must keep it, so that your fame may endure for ever." The king went back sadly to his room. That evening Bijal came and played a melody, of which the charm was more terrible than any that the king had yet heard. At last Dyach rose in despair and drawing his sword sheared off his own head with a single blow. The boy picked it up, and wrapping his fiddle in his cloak, went with the head to Ajmir, where lived king Anira.

The news of his deed had gone before Bijal; so when king Anira learnt that he was come near Ajmir, he sent his men and bade them beat him and drive him forth from the kingdom. "He caught in his snare," he cried, "the greatest king in all India; if I let him come to Ajmir, he will kill me, as he killed King Dyach." So King Anira's soldiers beat Bijal and drove him out into the desert, warning him that if ever he came back, they would kill him in spite of his music.

Bijal went to his village, and calling his wife took her with him back to the Girnar. As he neared it, he saw a great crowd outside the city, and learnt that King Dyach's wife, Surat, was about to commit suttee. He stood and watched. As he watched, Surat mounted a great pyre, which she had caused to be made ready. Then Queen Khatu mounted by her side and the two queens bade their attendants light the pyre. A great remorse seized Bijal, when he saw the sorrow that he had brought on King

Dyach's house; and as the flames rose, he rushed past the attendants and flung himself into the burning mass. Then Bijal's wife knew that by taking King Anira's jewels she had led her husband to his death, and in an agony of grief she too threw herself into the flames.

Momul and Rano

Once upon a time there lived in Sind a king, Nanda by name. He had a wonderful pig's tooth which had the power of drying up water, if put close to it. King Nanda used the pig's tooth in this way. He took it to the Indus, and putting the tooth close to the surface of the water, dried up the great river. Whenever King Nanda wanted money, he would go to the bank of the Indus and dry it up with his magical tooth, take from it such treasure as he needed, and return home. When he took the pig's tooth away, the river began to flow once more.

Now it so happened that an anchorite learnt about the pig's tooth by means of his inner knowledge. Filled with greed, he went to the king's palace when Nanda was absent. King Nanda had nine daughters of whom Momul was the most beautiful, and the wisest, Somal. When the anchorite reached the palace, he began to weep and moan and groan so loudly that his cries roused the princesses. Unhappily the wise Somal, who would have seen through the anchorite's pretence, had gone away with King Nanda.

As it was, the beautiful Momul sent for the anchorite and asked him what ailed him. He told her that he was very ill and like to die, but could he but get a pig's tooth, he would at once get well. Momul remembered that her father, the king, had a pig's tooth. Not knowing its magical properties, she took it from Nanda's room and gave it to the stranger. The anchorite took it and instantly recovered from his feigned illness. Then, going to the bank of the Indus, he dried up its waters, dug out a treasure, and travelling to a distant city spent the rest of his life there, in great peace and happiness.

When King Nanda came back with his daughter Somal and learnt that Momul had given his pig's tooth to a wandering anchorite, he was so angry that he would have killed Momul, had not his wise daughter Somal soothed him by saying that she knew a way in which Momul could get back just as big a treasure as the anchorite had stolen. Next day she took Momul to a spot far out on the Sind "pat" or desert, and there by her sorcery she created a beautiful palace and round it a garden blooming with flowers, and fragrant with fruit. In front of the garden she laid out a maze, round which there seemed to flow a great red river, which she named the Kak. Leading into the maze was a tunnel. Inside the tunnel Somal put by means of her sorcery terrible contrivances which roared and screamed at her will. At each corner of the magic palace she chained a lion, ready to tear in pieces, anyone who sought to enter. When her task was done, she called Momul, and bade her and her slave-girls live in the palace and proclaim that she would wed the first man who could find his way through the tunnel and maze to her chamber.

Now such was Momul's beauty that all the princes and nobles of Sind, taking with them their treasure and their men-servants, went forth gaily to win the lovely princess. As the wooers came to the outer gate, Momul sent her slave-girls to greet them and invite them to try to win her hand. Led by the slave-girls, they one by one entered the tunnel and passed into the maze. Then the magic river Kak circled round the maze closing all exit, so that the wooers died miserably, one after the other, and the princess's slaves stripped their bodies and plundered their treasure. A few only, whose hearts failed them in the tunnel or who fled back from the maze before the Kak river surrounded it, wholly escaped; but they found that in their absence Momul's slaves had taken their tents and their horses.

Now about this time there ruled in Umatkot, King Hamir, a Rajput of the Sumro clan. He had three viziers, all devoted to one another and still more to King Hamir. Nor would the king ever go hunting or to battle unless either Dunar or Shinro or Rano rode at his side. All four were as handsome and brave as could be, but the handsomest and bravest was Rano.

One day the king and his viziers went a-hunting. As they came near to a village, they saw a beggar-man standing by the road-side. His face and bearing were those of a man gently born, but he was covered with rags and half-dead with want and wretchedness. At first the four young men laughed at his strange appearance. Then they went up to him and asked him who he was and whence he came. "You seem to be gently born," said King Hamir, "yet I have never seen anyone in such a sorry state." The beggar answered courteously, "My lord king, there was a time when I was rich as anyone of the three nobles by your side. I had horses and lands and a host of attendants. But one day, to my sorrow, I heard of the beauty of princess Momul, and with a great store of gold and a troop of companions I set forth to win her. But she and her slaves murdered all my friends and plundered me of even my horse, so that I am now begging my way back to my own country."

The king asked who Momul was, and the beggar-man told her the story. After hearing it, the king and his three viziers vowed that they too would try to win her, or would die in the attempt. They asked the beggar-man the way to her palace, and after several days' journey they reached the outer gate of her garden, just as it was growing dark. They camped there for the night, and next morning one of Momul's slave-girls came to greet them. Her name was Natar, and she was so pretty and graceful that at first the four young men thought that she must be Momul herself. But Natar laughed, and said, "Nay, I am not the princess. To see her, you must win through to the palace. No man except her father has yet seen her face. But she sent me to welcome you and offer you this tray of food." She put down the tray on the ground; and as the young men ate the food, she described to them Momul's beauty, until they all grew sick with love. Then she mocked them, saying, "Who are you to think of my lovely princess? The hero who would win her must be cast in a different mould. You had better run back to your villages. If not, you will be torn to pieces in the tunnel, or die of hunger and thirst in her maze." In this way Natar excited their desire and their courage, until they all cried together that they feared neither the tunnel nor the maze, but that they would stay by Momul's gate until they bore off in triumph the beautiful maiden. In answer, the slave-girl threw them a tangled skein of silk and said, "Test your skill by undoing this, before you try to find your way through the maze." King Hamir took the skein; first he, and then Dunar, and then Shinro tried in vain to unravel it. At last they passed it on to Rano. His deft fingers soon solved the knot, and untying it he made the silken skein into a tassel and fastened it as a plume to his horse's head.

The slave-girl looked at Rano in wonder; then she went back to her mistress, and said, "Four beautiful youths have come to win you, but one, Rano by name, is fairer and wiser than the others, or indeed than any wooer who has yet come to your palace-door. Why not marry him, my mistress, at once? Do not kill this gallant as you have killed the others." The princess felt a moment's pity. Then she hardened her heart and answered. "If, forsooth, he is as wise as you say, let him win me. If he fails, he is but a fool, and I shall add his wealth to my father's treasure."

Then she got ready some tasty dishes, and put a deadly poison in each of them: giving them to the slave-girl, she bade her take them back to the king and his three viziers. The slave-girl did so; and setting the tray before them, served each of them with her own hands, saying, "Fair sirs, my mistress has cooked these dishes with her own hands for you as she fears that you must be weary after trying to unravel the skein." The king and Shinro and Dunar would have eaten the food and perished miserably, had not Rano thrown a piece to a stray dog. The dog ate it, and at once rolled over screaming in agony. The king rose in wrath and said to his viziers, "We will go back to our homes and let this murderess be." But Rano replied, "O! king, to go back now would be the act of cowards. Let us go on with our task; and, with God's help, we shall win the maiden."

In the meantime, Natar went back to the palace and told Momul how Rano had saved his comrades from the poison. She again pleaded with her mistress to spare him. But the princess rebuked her, saying, "If I spared him, all men would laugh at me. Go now to the young men, and invite them, one by one, to win through to my chamber. When they have entered the maze, they will fall easy victims."

Natar did as her mistress ordered. Going to King Hamir, she said, "Come with me, King Hamir. My princess challenges you to win her. If you but find your way to her chamber, she is yours."

The king rose to his feet and followed the slave-girl into the tunnel. There, in the darkness, she slipped away, leaving the king alone. The contrivances created by Somal's magic began to roar and scream, imitating the cries of wild beasts and the hissing of snakes, and filing the whole air with horror. The king all but fainted. Had he fainted outright, he would have been lost; for the princess's slaves were lurking near, and they would have fallen on him and killed and robbed him. But he recovered himself; and giving up the quest, made his way back to where his comrades sat waiting. He told them of the horrors of the tunnel and of the awful noises that he had heard there. "Let us stay here no longer," he said to his viziers. "Let us go back to Umarkot."

But Rano said: "My lord king, although you have failed, you have tried; and so none can blame you. But if we go back without even trying, all Umarkot will laugh us to scorn. Let us all try. Then if we fail, we can go back together."

Just then Natar came to the camp, and said with a mocking smile, "You stayed in the princess's garden but a short time, King Hamir. You will never win Momul thus. Now, who among your viziers will come with me to seek her?"

Dunar rose and mounted his horse and followed Natar into the tunnel. There she slipped away; and all round Dunar, Somal's contrivances began to hiss and roar and scream. Dunar's heart failed him: and turning his horse's head, he galloped back trembling to the king's camp, and told his comrades what had befallen him.

A few minutes later, Natar came out of the garden and said scornfully, "King Hamir, your vizier stayed on the quest even less time than you did. Hearts so faint will never win so fair a lady."

Then Shinro rose and donned his armour; and mounting a chestnut horse, he followed Natar into the tunnel. But he too lost heart, and galloped back before entering the maze.

At last Rano rose to try his fortune. While the others in vain sought to dissuade him, Natar came to the camp; and her lips curled with scorn, as she said, "It is but waste of time to lead you into my mistress's garden. You are all cowards, impostors! At the first sound you run away like frightened hares. Such cravens will never win Momul and her beauty."

Rano donned his armour and mounted a dun horse; and praying to Heaven to help him, he followed Natar into the tunnel. There he seized her, so that she should not leave him: and he held her firmly, while Momul's hellish machines roared and screamed all round him, until his ears were deafened with the noise and his eyes blinded with the darkness. The cunning slave-girl, finding that she could not free herself, led Rano to the edge of a pit. There she gave his horse a push, so that it fell into the pit, carrying its rider with it. As Rano fell, he heard the slave-girl laugh scornfully at him out of the darkness.

Happily, the horse fell under the youth, so that he was not badly hurt by the fall. He clambered out, and made his way from the tunnel into the maze. As soon as Rano was inside the maze, the waters of the Kak river closed round it, so that whenever he came to the edge of the maze, he found a raging torrent in front of him. To test its force, he threw into it an areca-nut. But the nut, instead of floating, bounded along the surface of the stream. Then Rano guessed that the Kak river was but an illusion, and that the ground in front of him was only part of the dry desert. So he walked to the edge of the river, and stepped boldly into it. At once the river vanished; and Rano, walking on, found himself close to Momul's palace.

The lions in the palace-courtyard crouched as if to spring on the youth, while, from the window, the princess screamed and scolded at him: but drawing his sword, he rushed past the lions and through the palace-door. Then he ran upstairs into the room where he had seen the princess. She no longer screamed or scolded. Directly he entered the room, she ran towards him and threw herself into his arms, crying, "You have won me fairly, bold prince! Take me! I am yours."

II

When morning broke, Rano took leave of the princess. At first Momul would not hear of his going. Indeed, it was not until he had promised to return every night, that, with many tears and embraces, she let her lover go. He put on his armour, mounted his dun horse, and rode back through the maze and the tunnel until he reached King Hamir's camp. There a cry of joy greeted him from Hamir and his two viziers; for they had made sure that Rano had perished in the tunnel, and they had been grieving for him as for one dead. "Where have you been?" "Why did you tarry so long?" "Did you win your way to the magic palace?" Such were the questions that met him on his return.

Rano feared the king's jealous wrath; so he answered with downcast eyes that he too had failed. "All right," he said, "I wandered in that accursed tunnel, and only now I have escaped."

Shinro and Dunar believed him; but the king suspected Rano's words to be false, for his bearing was not that of a man who had failed in a high adventure. "My comrades," said the king, "as we have all failed, let us go back to Umarkot; but let none of us say aught to any man, or the shame of our failure will resound throughout India."

The king and his three viziers rode back silently to Umarkot; for Hamir was angry with Rano, Shinro and Dunar were sad at their ill success, and Rano feared the wrath of his master.

On reaching Umarkot, Rano at once bethought him of his promise to Momul. That very night, and every night afterwards, Rano mounted a wonderful she-camel that he had; in an hour's time she brought him from Umarkot to the princess's palace. Before dawn, he rose and bade Momul good-bye; before daylight, he was back in his own house. This he did night after night for several weeks; but all the time the king's anger was burning more and more fiercely, until at last he refused to speak to Rano or acknowledge his salute, and he thought only how he might bring about Rano's ruin.

At last Rano sought a private audience of the king. He confessed to him that he had lied, and begged his mercy. "Tell me what really happened," said King Hamir, "and I will forgive you." Rano told the king the whole truth; how he had won through the tunnel and the maze; how he had crossed the magic river, and how, sword in hand, he had forced his way into Momul's room. Then he described the beauty of Momul with such glowing words, that King Hamir longed to see her more than ever. "Let me see her but once," he cried, "and I will give back to you all my former favour."

Rano thought for a moment; then he said, "She will not see you, King Hamir, if you come as a king; but if you come disguised as my servant, she will suspect nothing, and you will see her."

So King Hamir disguised himself as a cowherd. He put on an old garment that reached his feet, he tied a scarf round his head, and he took a stick in his hand. Then he got up behind Rano on his swift camel, and in an hour's time they had reached the outer gate of Momul's garden. Rano guided the camel through the tunnel and the maze, across the river, and into Momul's courtyard. There he made the camel kneel, and flinging the nose-string to King Hamir, he walked into the palace and up the stairs into Momul's room. Momul asked who the man was whom he had brought with him. "He is only a cowherd," said Rano. But Momul answered, "If he is only a cowherd, how comes it that he is so fair?" "He is the son of a slave-girl," said Rano, "and he was brought up in my father's house." But Momul suspected that the stranger was no herdsman. To test him, she had a she-buffalo brought into the courtyard and bade him milk it. Then she turned into the palace with Rano, and both forgot all else but each other's love.

King Hamir milked the she-buffalo as best as he could, but his body itched and his hands grew red with the unwonted labour: and all the time his wrath grew fiercer against Rano, whom he knew to be in the arms of the lovely woman, who had spoken to him so curtly. Every minute seemed a month, until at last his growlings and cursings reached the ears of Rano upstairs. He rose and, bidding Momul farewell, went back to the courtyard and tried to soothe the king. But Hamir's anger would not be appeased. Sullenly he rode back with Rano to Umarkot, and, as soon as they reached the city, flung him into prison. There he remained in a noisome cell for seven days and nights. On the eighth day his sister, the most beautiful of King Hamir's wives, begged the king to release her brother. At first Hamir refused; but at last he said, "Tomorrow I will ask him a riddle. If he guesses it, he shall be a free man. If not, he shall go to the gallows." It was in vain that Rano's sister tried to make the terms less hard.

Next morning Rano was led in chains to the royal palace. The king turned on him an evil look, and said, "I have a riddle to ask you. If you guess it, you are a free man. If you fail to guess it, you die this very day." "As the king pleases," said Rano. "Ask me the riddle that I may know my fate." "The riddle," said King Hamir, "is this:

"How came the wide rent in the sari of silk?"

Now Rano's wisdom had already been proved in his quest of Momul; so, after but a moment's hesitation, he answered:

"The king toyed with his wife, whose child newly born
Cried to its mother to give it some milk:
She jumped to her feet, and her sari was torn."

Hamir was amazed at the ready wit of his vizier, and at once set him free and gave him back all, and more than all, his old honours; and every night as before, Rano mounted his camel and rode to the princess's fairy palace.

At last, it fell out that Rano's wife and his father Kabir began to suspect Rano's intrigue. Rano's wife noticed red dust on her husband's clothes, whereas the dust of Umarkot was white. Rumours of Momul's love for Rano had spread over the countryside, and reached Kabir. He wondered how Rano could go to Momul's palace, and return in one night for it was two hundred miles from Umarkot. He went to Rano's stables and there learnt of the exceeding swiftness of Rano's she-camel. He at once ordered her to be taken out of the stables and killed. Then he had her buried in a distant pit.

That night, when Rano looked for his she-camel, he could not find her. Nor could he find his camel-men; for they had fled, when Kamir led the she-camel away to kill her. At last he found a deaf camel-man, who had stayed behind. He bawled in his ears, "Where is my she-camel?" The deaf man answered, "Your father killed her; but she had a young camel, and it will carry you just as swiftly." With these words he took Rano to the young camel's stable. They led it out, petted it; and promised it rich food, if it carried Rano well. Then they bridled and saddled it; and it carried Rano even more swiftly than its mother had done. Thus he reached Momul's house at the appointed time.

But Rano did not spend all night with Momul as he had done before. Instead, he returned home early and, having cleaned his clothes, sought his wife's couch, so that she might not suspect him. So Rano's wife and his father thought that Rano no longer visited Momul.

Unhappily, the tale of Momul's love for Rano reached the ears of the queen, her mother, and of her sister Somal. The queen grieved for her daughter's good name; but Somal grieved because Momul no longer snared and robbed young men, that she might repay to King Nanda his lost treasure. Somal thought of a cruel trick. She went to Momul's palace and greeted her sister with feigned affection. Then she vowed that she must sleep with her on the same couch. When her sister had gone to sleep, Somal slipped from her side, and, exchanging her clothes for those of a man, again lay down by Momul's side.

In the meantime, Rano was speeding on his swift camel through the night to his beloved. As he went, he strayed some distance from the path, and meeting a camel-man, asked him the way to Momul's palace. Now the camel-man had been specially sent by Somal to wait for Rano: so he answered, "Do you mean King Nanda's daughter, Momul, the mistress of Sital?" Then he showed Rano the way. Rano heard the lying words, but he thought no more of them, for he felt sure of Momul's love. He reached the palace, and, running upstairs, opened the door of Momul's room. By her side lay a young man asleep.

Rano's first impulse was to draw his sword and kill the guilty pair. But when he looked at Momul's sleeping face, he had not the heart to hurt her: so he put by her side his camel-switch, and then, going softly downstairs, mounted his camel, and rode back to Umarkot.

When Momul woke next morning, she saw by her side Rano's camel-switch. Going into the courtyard, she saw the tracks of his camel both coming and going. Then she guessed that Rano had come during the night, and, seeing her in Somal's arms, had thought her faithless and had gone away. She sent him a message begging him to come back to her and telling him that the man whom he had seen sleeping, as he thought, at her side, was not a man at all, but her sister Somal. But Rano bade the messenger tell Momul that he could not disbelieve what he had himself seen, and that no woman would have worn a man's clothes. Momul sent a second messenger explaining the true facts, and many others afterwards. But Rano would not believe them; and at last he bade the messenger repeat to her these words, "I will never forgive you, Momul, not though you come to my door as a beggar to ask my pardon."

When the messenger gave Momul this message, she was at first overcome with grief: then she dressed herself like a sanyasi in a saffron robe, and, with a begging-bowl and a staff in her hands, went begging from village to village until she reached Umarkot. There she went to Rano's house and asked for alms. The young vizier did not pierce her disguise, but, being attracted by her face, asked, "Whence have you come, holy sir? When did you become a sanyasi? Were you brought up in this holy state, or did you grow weary of the world and, become the pupil of some saint?" "Nay, fair youth," replied the sanyasi, "I am no man's pupil. I have learnt all the wisdom that man can teach, and I am myself a guru; so give me alms in the name of God." Rano was greatly pleased by the reply, and bade the anchorite enter his house. Momul did so, and for many days she stayed with Rano as his honoured guest.

One day Rano challenged Momul to a game of dice, and asked her what the stakes should be. "If I win," said Momul, "I shall stay with you always. If I lose, I go away to-morrow." "As you please," answered Rano laughing; and the two sat down to the game. Rano made his throw, and Momul lifted her arm to make hers. Unhappily, in doing so, she bared her arm, and Rano saw on it a mole, which he had often noticed on Momul's arm. He rose and in a harsh voice bade her begone. She threw aside her saffron robe, hoping that he would melt at the sight of the form that he had once so often embraced. But he pushed her out of the house and into the street, and shut the door in her face.

Momul, broken-hearted, went out from the town, and hiring villagers to help her, built a great pyre in the plain. Then she mounted it and set fire to it with her own hands. The news that a suttee was burning herself outside the town reached Rano's ears, and he went to see. The sight of Momul about to die filled him with remorse, and he cried to her, "Momul, come back to me. I was wrong. I believe you," But Momul shook her head, and said, "Dear one! Now that you know I was true to you, I need no further happiness. You love me now; so let me die. Were I to live longer, you might again mistrust me."

When she had spoken, the pyre fell inwards, and a great sheet of flame wrapped the princess round and consumed her. Then the memory of her beauty came back to Rano, and he felt that without Momul his life was worth nothing. Going close to the burning pyre, he sprang upon the spot where Momul had vanished in the flames. Thus in death the lovers were united.

Saif-ul-Mulk

Once upon a time King Hashimshah, son of Safian, ruled in Egypt. He was rich and powerful, and his subjects were happy. But he had no son. When young, he had not cared so much; but when he was seventy years old, he became so sad at his childlessness, that suddenly he shut himself up in his palace and refused to see either his ministers or his nobles. At last the business of the kingdom stopped altogether. With the courage of despair, the prime minister Saleh disobeyed the king's orders, and forcing his way into the royal presence, said respectfully, "My lord king, what is your trouble? If you will but tell it to me, I am sure I can cure it." "My good Saleh," answered the king, "it is no ordinary trouble. My treasury is full and my army is invincible. But I have no son to follow me on the throne of Egypt." "My lord king," said the vizier, "send for your astrologers. They will find in the stars the remedy for your sorrows."

Next morning the king sent for his astrologers, and bade them declare how he might get a son. The astrologers went away to consult the stars; three days later they came back, and said, "If the king marries the daughter of Sharaf Shah, King of Yemen, she, so say the stars, will bear him a son."

King Hashimshah at once sent an embassy to Yemen with fifty camels laden with pearls, four hundred pretty slave-girls, and an equal number of beautiful horses, as a gift to the King of Yemen. When the embassy came near Yemen, Sharaf Shah's soldiers rode out to ask whether they came for war or peace. The envoys replied that they had come to ask for the hand of the king's daughter; and the soldiers thereupon led them into the presence of the king. The envoys gave King Sharaf Shah their credentials, and, when he read King Hashimshah's letter, he cried out, "If I had seven daughters instead of one, he should wed them all!" He then sent for his daughter and married her to a sword and turban.

Soon after, the embassy let Yemen, to conduct the princess to King Hashimshah. By the princess's request, she was accompanied by her friend, the vizier's daughter. When they reached Egypt, King Hashimshah married the princess, and gave her friend as wife to Saleh, his prime minister. In less than a year both brides had become mothers. King Hashimshah called his son Saif-ul-Mulk, while the prime minister named his son Sayad; and the two little boys were nursed by the same nurse, and were brought up together like twin brothers.

When the boys were fourteen years old, the king sent for them, and gave to his son a ring and a robe which had once belonged to King Solomon. To Sayad he gave a horse and a tunic. That night the prince woke up and unfolded the robe given by his father. Instantly he saw close to him the most beautiful girl in the world. But when he put out his hands to catch her, she vanished. When he dropped his hands, he saw her again. At last he folded up the robe and put it away, but, for love of the beautiful maid, be could not sleep all night. Next morning the king noticed that the prince did not go a-hunting, and sent for him. But the prince would not reply to his father's questions. He could think of nothing but the lovely girl whom he had seen at night; and, at every question, he shook his head and wept bitterly. King Hashimshah was in despair. He sent for his doctors; but they could not cure the prince. At last the prime minister said, "Let my son try; he will go to the prince when he is alone, and he will threaten to kill himself, if needs be, unless the prince reveals his trouble." The king agreed, and Sayad went to the prince and implored him to unburden his heart, as to a brother. Touched with Sayad's devotion, the prince found his tongue and told him of the beautiful vision that he had seen, and how he loved it. Sayad repeated his story to the king, who, when he heard it, exclaimed, "Once, when I was a young man, I was sitting on my throne. Suddenly there was a flash of lightning, followed by a clap of thunder; and seven fairies dropped from the sky to the earth close by my feet. They gave me the robe and the ring that I gave the prince, and they said that these had once belonged to King Solomon. I opened the robe, and I saw standing in front of me the most beautiful girl in the world; but when I held out my hands to her, she vanished. I asked the fairies who she was. The seven fairies said, 'She is Badia-ul-Jamal, the daughter of Shahwal, king of the fairies, who lives in the town of Gulistan Aran.' On hearing this, I sent men out everywhere to find Gulistan Aran; but none could. I remained in love with her for fourteen years, and now she has cast her spell over my son. I will send out four hundred nobles in different directions, to seek her."

The king's nobles went to Persia, to India, to Arabia, to Afghanistan, to Turkestan, and many other lands, without finding

Gulistan Aran. The prince, partially recovered his spirits, when the nobles set forth; but when all returned unsuccessful, he fell back into his former state. The king then felt that the prince, if he was not to die of melancholy, must go himself and look for his beloved. He made vast preparations. He had ships built and provisions for five years stored in them. One ship was reserved for the prince and Sayad: in others sailed sixty nobles, whom the king placed on duty with his son.

In forty days' time the prince with his nobles reached the shores of China. When Fazfir, the King of China, heard that some ships were anchored off his coast, he sent an envoy on board to ask them who they were and why they had come. The prince replied that they had come in search of the country of Gulistan Aran. The envoy repeated to the king the prince's words. King Fazfir sent for the prince, and welcoming him cordially, promised to help him in his search. He asked all his courtiers and made inquiries everywhere, until at last he found an old man who said that as a child he had heard that Gulistan Aran was a month's journey distant.

When the prince heard this, he took leave of the king of China, and after thanking him warmly, weighed anchor and sailed in the direction given him by the old man. When they were near the end of the voyage, a typhoon caught the ships, all of which broke in pieces and foundered. The prince escaped in a boat with four or five sailors, and with great difficulty reached the coast. For three days and nights he and the men with him wandered about without meeting anyone. At last they saw a village in the distance and made their way towards it. But the villagers, who were ogres and cannibals, rushed out and seized them and took them before their king. The king would then and there have killed and eaten them, had his daughter Arbal not fallen in love with prince Saif-ul-Mulk. She begged her father to spare his life and the lives of his companions. The king at first refused, but in the end yielded to her entreaties. "Unbind the prince," he said: "he is to be the husband of my daughter, Princess Arbal."

On hearing these words, the prince felt his heart sink within him, for Arbal, although quite young, was ugly beyond description. Her head was as round and big as the dome of a mosque: her voice was like a dog's bark: she was covered with hair: her ears were as big as flowerpots: her lower lip hung down like a camel's: and her skin was jet black. That night Arbal sent for the prince, but he could not bear to go near her. His refusal made her very angry; and she had the prince and his companions put in chains, until the king should be pleased to kill and eat them.

The prince told his companions what fate was in store for them. So they bided their time; and one day they broke their chains, seized a boat, and in it made for the open sea. At last they reached an island full of fruits, that seemed luscious to the castaways. They ate great quantities; but the fruits were poisonous, and that night all except Saif-ul-Mulk died of the poison.

Saif-ul-Mulk, who had eaten sparingly, was deadly ill; but he recovered. As the day wore on, his strength returned: and when he had buried his fellow-travellers, he walked about exploring the island. Suddenly he heard behind him the rush of mighty wings, and, before he could flee to shelter, a giran[†] bird swooped down on him and carried him off to its nest, to feed its young ones. Saif-ul-Mulk had given up all hope and had commended his soul to Allah, when he saw a gigantic snake ascending the tree on which was the giran bird's nest. The bird was so delighted with its prey, that it did not see the snake; and it was about to drive

---

[†] A giant eagle.

its cruel beak into Saif-ul-Mulk's breast and tear out his vitals,
when it was itself seized by the giant python. The mighty bird
fluttered and screamed, but the python never relaxed its grip:
fastening its coils round the giran's body, it crushed it, so that
the prince heard its bones crack. Then, having swallowed its
victim whole, the snake went down the tree again.

The prince was for some time too frightened to stir: but when
he could no longer see the snake, he slipped down the tree, and
ran, as hard as he could, to another part of the island. At last
he came to a palace: in front of the door lay a huge lion asleep.
Saif-ul-Mulk drew his sword, and, going up to the sleeping brute,
drove his blade deep into its heart. It rolled over dead; and the
prince, striding over its body, entered the palace. He passed
through three rooms all beautifully furnished and full of rich
ornaments; and in the fourth he saw a splendid golden throne
studded with jewels. The throne was turned away from him; but
when he went in front of it, he saw a maid seated upon it, fast
asleep. She was as lovely as the maiden whom he had seen, when
he opened the robe of King Solomon. Stepping to her side, he
boldly kissed her cheek. The beautiful girl opened her eyes and
smiled: then she said, "Who are you, young sir, that you dare
come into this land of Devs?"

The prince shook his head and said, "My tale is far too long
to tell; but who are you, and why do you lie sleeping here,
although the sun is high in the heavens?"

The fair maid answered, "My name is Mulkan, and I am a
king's daughter. One day I went with my companions to my
father's garden, and with them bathed in the lake. Suddenly a
mighty wind blew, and it carried me off from the shore of the
lake to this island. I reached the ground in front of this palace
wherein lives the king of the island, who is a Dev. He came to

me, surrounded by a number of other Devs, and told me that he had carried me off because he loved me. He said that it was useless for me to resist his advances, since my home and parents were far away, and neither man, bird nor animal could reach his island-stronghold. Then he made me sit down on this throne, where I at once fell asleep. Every morning he wakes me up, gives me food, and talks to me. Then he goes out with other Devs, and I at once fall asleep again, and remain asleep until he comes next day. In this way more than a month has passed. But now tell me who you are. There is time enough for the longest story: the Dev will not come until to-morrow morning."

The prince related how he had set out to find Badia-ul-Zamal, and all the hazards through which he had passed since he had left his father's kingdom. The princess Mulkan clapped her hands with delight, when she heard that Saif-ul-Mulk was in love with Badia-ul-Zamal. "Why, she is my sister!" she cried, "If you can only save me from the clutches of this hateful Dev, my parents will surely reward you with my sister's hand."

The prince and the princess talked together all that evening and far into the night, planning how they might flee to Gulistan Aran. At last the prince said, "Ask the Dev king where he keeps his life. For Devs do not keep their lives in their bodies as we do. If you can learn from him where his life is, I will find out its hiding-place and destroy it."

The princess agreed. Not long afterwards she looked at the sky and said, "My brother, the east is beginning to pale. The Dev will come back soon. Go now and return this evening." The prince departed, and the princess at once fell fast asleep again.

That evening the prince returned to the palace and found the princess sleeping, as before, on the golden throne. He kissed her cheek, and she woke up. Seeing the prince, she cried gladly, "I have found out where the Dev keeps his life hidden. At first when I asked him, he flew into a rage. But I coaxed and wheedled and flattered him so artfully, that at last he told me that he kept his life locked up in a box buried at the foot of a tree across the river. But alas! he also said that no one could ever find the box unless he had the ring of King Solomon: so how will you be able to find it?"

The prince answered joyfully, "Because I have the ring of King Solomon;" and he told the princess how he had come by it. Then, running out of the palace, he went straight to the tree, beneath which was the box in which the Dev's life was hidden. He opened the lid, and saw a dove inside and a quantity of precious stone. Guessing the dove to be the Dev's life, he seized it with one hand, and with the other he cut his head off. He took the precious stones with him, and ran back to the palace; then, with the princess, he boarded a little ship, which lay near the shore and had belonged to the Dev.

They set sail for the open sea; and, after perils and hardships too many and too great to be recounted, the prince steered the ship safely to the coast of Gulistan Aran. He landed, leaving the princess in the boat, and went inland to explore. Presently he met a man who seemed in search of something that he had lost. The prince questioned him, and he replied, "Some months ago the Princess Mulkan was carried away by a whirl wind, and never returned. I and many others are looking for her day and night, but cannot find her."

The prince said nothing in reply, but he returned to Mulkan and told her what the man had said. The princess clapped her hands with joy, and cried, "Thanks be to Allah! This is indeed my own land. Let us go at once to the nearest town and ask news of my father."

Mulkan led the way to the nearest town, and there she and the prince asked for an audience with the governor. But their clothes were so tattered and torn, that no one would admit them to the governor's palace. The prince was at his wit's end; but Mulkan wrote on a piece of paper the following words,—

"Like a dove, I have come back from a strange land to my own country; but my heart is full of sorrow."

Folding up the paper, she asked one of the sentries to take it to the governor. The governor opened the paper and read the curious words inside, but he could not understand them: so he bade the sentry call Saif-ul-Mulk. When the prince came in, the governor asked him who he was. The prince replied that he was a king's son, but that travel and hardship had made him look like a beggar. His bearing and countenance gave support to his words, and the governor asked him to tell his story. Then the prince related his adventures, and ended by saying that he had brought back the missing princess Mulkan.

When the governor heard this, he was overjoyed, for he was a kinsman of King Shahwal, the father of Mulkan and Badia-ul-Zamal. He sent a palki to fetch the princess with all ceremony, and then feasted her and the prince for many days, to celebrate her happy return.

Some days later the governor got up a hunt, to do the prince honour. As the prince was returning from the chase, he saw a man gathering fuel in a wood, who, so he fancied, was his former comrade, Sayad. The man was so worn with toil and exposure, that the prince could not be certain: so he sent some servants to fetch the fuel-gatherer to his house. The men, thinking Sayad had done the prince some injury, belaboured him soundly and dragged him, more dead than alive, to the prince's house.

"Who are you?" asked the prince sternly. Sayad was too frightened to recognise the prince. He threw himself at this feet, and said, "My lord, my name is Sayad. I was once the son of the vizier of Egypt and the friend of the king's son, but misfortune has made me what you see." The prince was now sure that the man was his former companion, and, lifting him to his feet, he embraced him tenderly, and bade him tell his story.

"When our ship foundered," said Sayad, "I contrived to swim to some wreckage, and, holding on to it, I was washed ashore. There I was seized by cannibals, who first resolved to kill me, but then decided to fatten me up and offer me as a fitting present to the king. For some days they fed me on a wonderful essence, which tasted of almonds but had the quality of making me enormously fat in a few days. Then they took me with them, to offer me to their king. Happily, on the way, we passed along the bank of a river: and suddenly freeing myself from my captors, I plunged into the stream. As they could not swim, I escaped easily to the further shore. In course of time I made my way to this country; and here I have been earning my livelihood by gathering sticks and selling them as firewood."

The prince, in turn, told Sayad what had befallen him: and after each had heard the other's story, they once more embraced one another and thanked Allah, who had brought them safely through so many perils.

In the meantime Mulkan's mother had heard of her return, and has come with a band of fairies to welcome her home. When they heard of her adventures and the prince's bravery, they resolved to see Saif-ul-Mulk themselves. They covered themselves with scent and ambergris and attar; and went off together to see the prince. They reached his house, just as he had finished telling Sayad his story. All the fairies admired the gallant bearing of the young man, but one fairy fell passionately in love with him. This was no other than Badia-ul-Zamal, Mulkan's sister and daughter of Shahwal, king of the fairies.

Badia-ul-Zamal said nothing to the prince then; but at night she could not sleep. At last she rose from her bed, stole softly to the prince's room, and kissed him as he slept. The prince woke and returned her embrace. After they had talked together for some time, Badia-ul-Zamal said softly, "I am a fairy; you are a man. I live here; you come from a distant land. If I marry you, you will soon grow weary of me and long to return home." The prince, however, vowed that he would never leave her; and at last Badia-ul-Zamal believed his vows.

Next morning the prince and Badia-ul-Zamal went to the princess Mulkan and afterwards to the governor. But the governor would not permit their marriage save with the consent of either King Shahwal or his sister, the Princess Sirobanu. As the princess lived nearer than the king, the governor wrote a letter, and told an Afrid to convey it and the prince to her palace, and so obtain her consent to the marriage.

The words had hardly left the governor's lips, when the prince felt himself caught up in the Afrid's arms, and transported through the air at incredible speed, high over valleys and mountains, rivers and plains. A moment later the Afrid put the prince down at the door of Sirobanu's palace. The prince induced one of the guards to take the governor's letter to the princess: and when she read it, she at once ordered the prince to be admitted to her presence. She received him graciously and listened in wonder to his adventures: finally she bade him stay in the palace, and feasted him there right royally.

Next morning the prince went out to bathe in a beautiful swimming bath, filled with rose-water, that lay at some little distance from the palace. After bathing, he lay down in the shade at the edge, and, fanned by the cool breeze, he soon fell asleep. As he slept, a hideous Dev swooped down from the sky, bore the prince away in his claws, and brought him to the king of the Devs. He, learning that the prince had compassed the death of the Dev who had held captive the Princess Mulkan, put him in-chains and threw him into a deep dungeon. When Saif-ul-Mulk did not return, the Princess Sirobanu had a search made everywhere for him, but in vain. She sent the Afrid to scour the heavens, and through his agency came to know the fate that had overtaken the prince.

The Princess Sirobanu made the Afrid take her to the court of King Shahwal. She told the king of fairies of the coming of the prince, how he had rescued Mulkan, how he had fallen in love with Badia-ul-Zamal, and how the Dev had carried him off out of her own pleasuregarden.

King Shahwal was unwilling to declare war on the Devs with whom the fairies were at peace. Moreover, he knew nothing of Saif-ul-Mulk, whom he had never seen. Princess Sirobanu was very angry at the king's indifference; she taunted him, but in vain. At last she sent the Afrid to fetch the Princess Badia-ul-Zamal. He did so, and Princess Sirobanu bade her join her entreaties to her own, so that King Shahwal might be moved to rescue the prince.

For some time King Shahwal would not alter his resolve. Then, seeing his daughter pine away at her lover's absence and the thought of his suffering, King Shahwal reluctantly sent a great army of fairies against the king of the Devs. Going with great speed into the country of the Devs, the fairies surprised their army, and took their king prisoner.

King Shahwal asked the captive king about Saif-ul-Mulk, but he would not confess where he had imprisoned him. At last King

Shahwal losts all patience, and ordered the prisoner's head to be struck off. Then the Dev king gave way; and, leading King Shahwal to his prisonhouse, he showed him the deep dungeon in which the prince had languished for four months.

Great then were the rejoicings of all; and King Shahwal ordered the prince and Badia-ul-Zamal to be married without delay. After some months of happiness the prince begged leave of King Shahwal to take his bride back to his own land of Egypt, and the king graciously agreed. He sent for the Afrid: and when he had presented the prince with great treasure, he entrusted him and Badia-ul-Zamal to the Afrid's care.

After the prince and the princess had bidden the kindly king and the Princess Sirobanu farewell, the Afrid rose with them into the heavens and began to fly in the direction of Egypt. When they had gone some little distance, the prince said to Badia-ul-Zamal, "Let us visit Mulkan on the way." The princess agreed, and the Afrid, with the speed of thought, brought them to earth in the Princess Mulkan's garden. The two sisters greeted each other fondly; and Badia-ul-Zamal learnt with great joy that, in Saif-ul-Mulk's absence, the Princess Mulkan and Sayad had fallen in love with each other and were betrothed. Indeed, the only hindrance to their marriage had been the prince's absence: for Sayad could not bear to be happy while his master's fate was unknown. Thus, when the Afrid brought the prince and his bride, the sole obstacle to Mulkan's and Sayad's marriage was removed, and it was celebrated without delay.

After the festivities were over, all four entrusted themselves to the Afrid's care; and he, lifting all four as easily as he had lifted two, flew with them on his back to Egypt. When they reached that country, King Hashim and his vizier, who had long mourned for their sons as dead, gave them a royal-greeting. The king poured out all his treasures in charity, and opened his granaries, and remitted a year's taxes, in honour of the prince's home-coming. Thus the prince and his faithful comrade, Sayad, reached Egypt safely with their brides, and they they lived happily for ever so long afterwards.

Umar and Marai

Once upon a time there ruled in Umarkot a famous king called Umar. He was a Rajput of the Sumro clan: and such was the splendour of his reign, that it would have restored their sight to the blind. Whether in the chase or in battle, he was as brave as a lion; and the justice of his rule was famous far and wide.

But all men, high or low, bad or good, rich or poor, must fulfil their destiny. Thus it came about that one day King Umar sat in his hall of audience, surrounded by his officers and governors: to all of them he gave a solemn warning that they should fear God and oppress no man. Suddenly, in front of the palace-gate, a stranger cried out that he craved a private audience with the king, as he had a message for his ears alone. When the king heard this, he dismissed his officers and governors, and received the stranger.

Now at the time that King Umar reigned at Umarkot, there lived in a village called Malir, in the Thar desert, a humble goatherd, named Palvi. He had a wife, named Merad, and a lovely daughter, called Marai. In their house also lived a servant, Phog by name, who aspired to Marai's hand. But Palvi had promised his daughter to her cousin Khet, whom she loved. So she rejected Phog's suit. In a fury, Phog left Malir, and, thirsting for vengeance, went to the palace-gate at Umarkot: he was the stranger who asked for, and obtained, an audience of King Umar.

When Phog was alone with the king, he said, "My lord king, I have a humble petition to make; and it is this. There lives in Malir a maiden, called Marai, whose beauty puts the sun to shame. Her form is tall and straight: her eyes are blacker than the humming bees: her glances are sharper than a soldier's sword: her skin is like satin: when she smiles, it is as if there fell a shower of pearls: her bosom is as white as the clouds in spring, and the buds there put to shame the rosebuds in your garden: her face is fairer than the moonbeam: her gait is like the pea-hen's: and, when she speaks, the 'coils' answer her from the forest. When a man has once seen her, he can look at naught else: yet she is but a goatherd's daughter, and in rags. If she were clad in fine raiment, she would be fairer than the 'peris'. Only you, O king, are fit to possess her. For if her form is lovely, her heart is a treasure-house of love. Come with me, and I will show you where she lives."

King Umar forgot all the noble words that he had just spoken to his officers and governors, and went mad with love for the goatherd's beautiful daughter. He had his fastest camel saddled, and, taking the reins, he mounted in front, while the treacherous servant sat behind him and showed him the way to Marai's village.

It so happened that Marai had gone with a girl-companion to fetch water at a well outside her village. Seeing a camel with two men riding upon it in the distance, she grew frightened and would have run back to her home. But the girl with her, curious to see the strangers, told her not to be afraid. "They are travellers," she said, "they will do you no harm. When they come to the well, they will ask for water. We will give it to them, and in return they will tell us all the news." Marai, persuaded by her companion, went on with her to the well, and reached it at the same time as Umar's camel. Phog's whisper and King Umar's own eyes told him that it was the beautiful Marai, who stood before him. He made his camel kneel, and alighting asked Marai for water. The simple girl was preparing to give him some, when suddenly Umar and Phog seized her and gagged her, and, tying her on the camel's back, took her away with them to the palace at Umarkot.

That night King Umar went to Marai and found her weeping. Her food lay untouched by her side. He tried to console her, saying, "Marai, do not weep. What is done, cannot be undone. You shall be my chief queen, and my other queens shall be your slaves. In your hands I will put the reins of my kingdom." But Marai only wept the more, as she thought of her home, of her parents, and of Khet, her affianced lover. Then King Umar said scornfully, "Why should you grieve for your parents and your lover, Marai? They are wild foresters. Here your word will be law to princes. In your village you have to rise at dawn and drive the goats in the sun; here you will live shaded and sheltered under the roof of my palace."

"Your ladies," retorted Marai, "think that it is a great thing to veil their faces and live behind palace-walls. But I love the open air and the sunshine on my face. I love the feel of a kid under each arm, as I go with the goats to the grazing-ground. I have nothing in common with your high-born beauties. They like dainty food: I live on wild fruit and berries. They have jewels round their necks: I wear a string of red beads. They love soft beds and bedding: I love to stretch myself on the cool sand. In their courtyards servants scatter water to lay the dust: but I love to feel the raindrops. They wear silk clothes: I wear coarse rags. They listen to the sound of your fifes and drums: but far sweeter to my ears is the bleating of my goats."

"But I will make you the fairest garden in all the world," said King Umar: "it shall be hung with gold lamps, and in it will grow vines and dates, plantains and limes, figs and oranges, cocoa-nuts and almonds; and the air will be heavy with the scent of areca-nut, cardamums, and sandalwood."

Marai shook her head, and answered, "Nay, keep those for others, King Umar: give me back the rough uplands that stretch round my village, and the brambles and thorn-bushes on the hills, and the fruit and wild berries that grow on them."

For many a night King Umar tried in vain to win Marai's love: but she was proof alike against tears, threats, and entreaties. One day he pitched a tent some miles from Umarkot, and bade herdsmen graze their cattle and goats round it, so that the sight of it might soften Marai's heart and make her smile on him. But Marai only laughed scornfully, and said, "Your trouble is wasted. The goats are like my village-goats, and the tent is like the tents in my village; but in the tent you should have put my parents, and the goatherd should have been my lover, Khet."

Then king Umar sent for a camel-man and bade him dress himself like a Malir peasant. Next he sent word to Marai that a man had come from her village with a message from her parents; and he asked leave to bring him to her room. Marai consented. When the man entered the room, he said, "Your mother has sent me to you: listen to her message, for these are her very words, "My daughter, why do you bring on us the hatred of King Umar by your obstinacy? All the world knows that he has taken you to his palace. Even though you remain chaste, the world will think you unchaste, so why refuse his love?" But Marai guessed the trick, and, as she looked sternly at the false messenger, he faltered and stammered beneath her gaze. "Love!" she repeated angrily: "there is no love but that blessed by heaven. No parents of mine would have sent me such a message. It is a black lie, which you have been bribed to tell me." When this scheme failed, King Umar strode out of the palace in a rage, vowing vengeance against Marai's parents and her lover; but for some time he left her in peace.

In the meantime Marai's parents had heard from her girl-companion how she had been carried off: but when they learnt later that the wrongdoer was no other than the great King Umar of Umarkot, they did nothing to rescue her. They fancied that her heart had yielded to the passion of the king and to the glamour of a royal palace.

But Marai's lover, Khet, distracted by her loss, went on foot to Umarkot and daily wandered in despair around her dwelling. Marai saw him, from her window and contrived to send him a message to be at a well-known shrine on a certain day with a swift camel. The next time King Umar came to see Marai, she soothed him by promising that if her parents and clansmen did not rescue her within a twelve-month of her capture, she would be his. By such soft words she got from him leave to visit the shrine on the day on which Khet was to meet her: and on the appointed day she and a crowd of richly dressed girl-companions went together to worship at the shrine. When they reached it, they got down from their palkis, and laughing and chattering and admiring each other's jewels, they paid little heed to a poorly dressed camel-man, who stood by a kneeling camel, not far from the saint's tomb. Suddenly, as they passed him, Marai left the group of heedless girls and ran to the kneeling camel as fast as she could. In a moment she and the camel-man, who was her lover, Khet, had jumped on its back, and the camel, rising to its feet, was soon racing towards Malir. The girls cried after her, "What are you doing, Marai? Why are you riding off with a stranger on a camel?" Marai called back mockingly, "Tell King Umar that on a camel I came, and on a camel I went."

The girl went back to their palkis, and, going home, told King Umar with trembling lips what had happened. The king was afraid to send an army into the desert to fetch Marai back, lest his nobles might upbraid him for doing injustice, when he bade others be just. So Marai reached her home safely. There she married her cousin Khet. Neither King Umar nor the wicked Phog ever came to trouble them again, and they lived happily ever after.

Kauro and Chanesar

Once upon a time there lived in Sind a great, rich lord, called Rao Khengar. Yet, with all his wealth and power, no prince in India was stricter in his observance of the Hindu faith, or was juster towards the subjects over whom he ruled. He had no son and only one daughter, Kauro. She was a beautiful girl: the court-poets likened her teeth to pearls, her bosom to pomegranates, her neck to a peacock's, and her walk to a pea-hen's. Spoilt by her father and praised by everyone, she used to deck herself in rich clothes, which she changed at least ten times a day. She would scent herself with ambergris, darken her eyes with antimony, and bathe herself in costly perfumes. But her chief joy was her necklace, in which shone two "shabchiragh"† stones, that at night-time lit up the whole palace with their cold, clear greenish light. Kauro was betrothed to a young kinsman, Itimadi by name; and Itimadi's sister, Jamna, was her constant companion.

---

† 'Shab' means 'night' and 'chirag' means lamp. They are two Persian words.

One day Jamna, seeing Kauro at her loom, which was old and worn, said to her, "That is no loom for you; with a rich father like yours, you should have a golden loom, studded with precious stones." Kauro was charmed with the idea, and instantly sent for the most skilled goldsmith in her father's town. Under her directions he made her in ten days a lovely loom all of gold and studded with rubies, each one as bright and red as the planet Mars. When the loom was ready, Kauro invited her girl-friends to her workroom, that they might see her golden loom. After they had all admired and praised it, they sad down to work at their own looms. But Kauro's delight at her new toy made her so restless, that she did nothing but strut about the room or gaze into the mirror, lost in admiration of her own beauty. The girls tried to tease her out of her folly, but she paid no heed to them. At last, as she strutted about her chamber looking over her shoulder at her looking-glass, she upset Jamna's loom and spoilt her work. Jamna, losing all patience, cried. "You are altogether too grand for my poor brother, Itimadi; you had better go and wed Chanesar."

Now Chanesar was the prince of Devalkot, and by far the greatest prince in all Rajputana. Kauro, stung to the quick by Jamna's gibe, flung out of the room and ran with streaming eyes to her mother, Marki; telling her what Jamna had said, she cried, "I will never marry that wretch's brother, Itimadi. I will wed King Chanesar and spite her."

Queen Marki at first tried to soothe her daughter; but at last she consented to break Kauro's betrothal with Itimadi, and to wed her to Chanesar.

The queen next went to Rao Khengar and induced him, sore against his will, to let her take her daughter to Chanesar's court. He collected camels and stores for their journey, and then sent Marki and Kauro off with five hundred horsemen to guard them, and four or five picked girl-slaves to serve the queen and princess.

The caravan set out for Devalkot, and often, as they rode towards Rajputana, the princess would pray to Heaven that she might win the great King Chanesar for her husband. On the way, the party crossed the lands of a robber-baron, called Sark, who, with his men, bade them halt and pay him tribute: but when he heard from the princess's messenger that she was a bride for the mighty Chanesar, he trembled and let them pass without paying toll.

Each day the princess asked anxiously of the villagers how far away Devalkot still was: at last a goat-herd told her that it lay only two day's march off. All were pleased at the news: and two days later they saw in the distance the city of their desire. The spoilt princess would have ridden boldly in and bidden King Chanesar marry her, but the wise old queen restrained her: "Nay, my daughter," she said, "you must be patient. Let us call ourselves horse-dealers, and, as much, we will spy out the land. But, as we shall want our horses, we will put such prices on them that no one will buy them."

As Marki advised, so they did. They camped near Devalkot, calling themselves horse-dealers: but although all Devalkot flocked to see their horses, their prices were so high that all turned away in disgust.

One day an old woman brought Kauro garlands of flowers for sale. The princess was so pleased with the flowers that she told the old woman her whole story from beginning to end, and begged her to devise some plan by which she might meet Chanesar. She promised, if the plan succeeded, to give the old woman anything she named. But the old woman shook her head: "I can do nothing," she said; "but if you tell the vizier, Jakro, he may be able to do what you ask." The princess took the old woman to her mother, and all three went together to the house of Jakro, the vizier. They told him the story, and the princess, throwing herself at his feet, begged and implored him to help her. At length the vizier was touched, and said, "Be of good heart! I will tell King Chanesar tomorrow, and I have every hope that he will send for you." With these words he dismissed the three women.

Next morning Jakro went to King Chanesar, and told him about the princess's visit: he pressed the king to send for her that he might see her beauty with his own eyes. But Chanesar answered coldly, "You know I have my queen Lila in my palace, and that I love her more than words can tell. How can you ask me to take this strange woman? Tell Kauro that she had better go back to her home, for I do not want her."

Jakro took this stern message back to Kauro. The princess said nothing until the vizier had gone: then she said to queen Marki, "I have only one chance of life left. I will die rather than go home unsuccessful; but perhaps, if we go to Lila herself, she may take pity on me and help me to meet Chanesar."

Then queen agreed, and mother and daughter went to Lila's palace. Lila asked them who they were, and why they had come. "We are strangers in the land," said Kauro, "and we have spent all our money. God has made you kind as well as great princess; so let us work in your house, we pray you. My mother can weave cotton as fine as the finest silk, and I am ready to do any task you give me."

Lila took pity on the two strangers, and, after asking their names, took them as servants; to Kauro she gave the work of daily spreading Chanesar's bedding; she bade Marki weave a turban for him.

One day tears began to flow down Kauro's cheeks, for she saw that, though the days passed, she came no nearer to meeting

Chanesar. Lila saw her tears and asked why she cried. "Princess," answered Kauro, "I am not crying, but the smoke of the lamp got into my eyes and they began to water. In my own house we never used lamps for the 'shabchiraghs' in my necklace lit it up from top to bottom." Lila laughed and said, "Show me your necklace and I will believe you." Kauro went and fetched her necklace from its case; and the cold green light of the two "shabchiraghs" radiated through the whole palace, and settled on Lila's heart like some deadly poison. "Ask what you like," cried the infatuated Lila: "ask what you like, but give me that wonderful necklace." "I want no money," answered Kauro; "only let me pass one night with your husband, Chanesar." Lila, blinded with her desire for Kauro's necklace, agreed at once. "Go to your house," she said, "and I will bring him to you this very evening."

Kauro went home and spread thick woollen carpets on the floor, and, so far as she could beautified for King Chanesar's reception the humble lodging that she and queen Marki had taken.

Now the king had that same evening gathered round him a number of his courtiers and comrades, and in their company he drank deep and revelled late, until at last his brain was wholly clouded with the fumes of wine. He rode back to Lila's palace, barely able to sit his horse. Lila came out to greet him, and seeing his condition rejoiced, for she thought that he would do anything she asked him. She went close to him, and said in wheedling tones, "My lord king, my handmaid, Kauro, is sick for love of you; go to her house and for this one night make her happy." Chanesar, drunk though he was, protested; but while he babbled, Lila's slave-girl took the reins of his horse and, turning the animal's head, led it to Kauro's door, before Chanesar was aware of what she was doing. There Kauro greeted the king, and, taking him by the hand, brought him into her room, where a Brahman hurriedly said over them the marriage "mantras." Then she took Chanesar in her arms, and told him again how much she loved him. But the drunken man only flung himself on his cot, and, turning his face to the wall, fell fast asleep. Kauro tried for an hour or more to rouse him: at last, in despair, she went to Marki's room, and bursting into tears cried, "Mother, what shall I do? Chanesar will not look at me or speak to me. He has turned his back on me; and nothing that I can do, will wake him." The queen answered, "But you *must* wake him. You bought him from Lila in exchange for your necklace."

Now it so chanced that just after Kauro left the room, Chanesar woke up: thus he heard the talk between her and her mother. When he realized that his queen Lila had sold him to Kauro for her necklace, he was furious. He called back Kauro, and, learning from her the whole story, he vowed that he would make her his queen in Lila's place. Next morning he gave a mighty feast in honour of his new bride. All that day Lila waited in vain for the king's coming: at last she sent a slave-girl to call him. But the king said to the slave-girl, "Go, tell your mistress that I am no longer her husband. Her husband is the necklace for which she sold me."

When Lila got the message, she went to the palace herself; but the door-keepers had orders not to let her in. She left the door, went away, and peeped through a little window, which looked into the king's private room. There she saw Chanesar and Kauro toying together, and the sight so hurt her that she fainted. When she became conscious, she dragged herself homewards and, covering her head with dust and beating her breast, she began to sob and scream at the top of her voice. All the women of the neighbourhood came running up; but when they heard that she had sold her husband for a single necklace, they laughed at her and went home.

At last, in despair, Lila went back to the palace, and, forcing her way past the door-keeper into Kauro's presence, scolded and upbraided her for her treachery. But Kauro only said with bitter scorn, "You cannot have loved your husband or you would not have sold him. Why not wear your necklace and make yourself happy in its society?" Then she told Lila to leave Devalkot at once or evil would befall her. The unhappy queen then begged Chanesar, as a last favour, to take her to her own home, so that her mother might console her. Chanesar agreed to go with her; but although they rode the same camel, he would not speak a single word to her. On the way they passed a herd of antelope. Chanesar, having made his camel kneel, stalked a buck and shot it. He then had a fire lighted, over which the buck was roasted. Lila hoped that he would give her some of the venison, as he had often done in old days when they had gone hunting together: but the king, after dividing the meat between himself and his followers, ate his own portion himself and gave the queen none. He then remounted his camel, and they rode again towards Lila's home. At some distance from her parents' town he halted, and, lifting Lila off the camel, bade her curtly good-bye. Then, turning his camel's head, he followed his men and servants, and rode as fast as he could to his own city.

Lila at first hoped against hope that Chanesar might return to her, but, as years passed and he made no sign, she despaired of ever seeing him again. One day the king's vizier, Jakro, became betrothed to one of Lila's kinswomen, and came to her village to wed her. Lila's mother heard of his arrival, and, going to her kinswoman's house, forbade the wedding. "No girl of my village," she said to Jakro, "shall wed a man of Devalkot, lest he treat her as Chanesar treated Lila." Jakro, in despair, went to Lila herself; and Lila, pitying him, said, "Nay, bring my beloved to your wedding, and it shall not be forbidden." Jakro rode back with all speed to Devalkot, and begged the king with folded hands to go with him. "I have served you all my life, my lord king," he said; "do me this favour now: otherwise they will never let me marry my betrothed."

Chanesar at first refused; but at last he yielded, and, with a brave escort of armed men, fifers and drummers, went with Jakro to Lila's village. As he drew near, Lila with the young women of the town, all closely veiled, went out to meet the king. At first she thought of throwing herself at his feet, but she feared that he might repulse her and all would laugh at her. So she went up to him, and said, "Welcome, my lord king, we hope you will choose a girl from our poor township; but if you do, pray do not treat her as you treated poor Lila." As she spoke, she laughed so merrily and tossed her head to saucily, that she caught the king's fancy; and, not recognising her, he replied, "Fair damsel, I will gladly take you back with me, if you will but come. But I pray you pull off your veil, that I may see your face; for I am sure it must be even sweeter to look at than your voice is to hear." Lila drew aside her veil, and said, "My lord king, see! I am Lila herself. I am she whom you flung aside for Kauro's sake. Take me; I am ready to come."

But as the words left her lips, Lila staggered and fell forward dead. The joy of meeting him whom she loved, had proved too great for her frame worn out with pain and sorrow. Then Chanesar, heartbroken at the sight, clasped his hands and prayed. "O God, I pray you take me too, for I cannot live without her." And God in his mercy heard the kings' prayer and granted it. A moment later the king had fallen dead across Lila's body.

Then Jakro, the vizier, had a pyre built, and placed the two bodies upon it, and the fire soon consumed them both. Thus, although Kauro had her way during Chanesar's life, it was Lila who went together with him into the valley of the shadow.

Rajbala

Rajbala was the daughter of Thakor Partabsing of Veshalpur, and throughout India had no rival in beauty or in wit, in wisdom or in daring. While she was still a child, her father had betrothed her to Ajitsing, son of Anarsing, a Soda Rajput who ruled in Umarkot.

Now Anarsing was king of but a small country, and, as he kept a large band of horsemen, he was forced to raid his neighbours' villages in order to pay them. One day it chanced that Anarsing's overlord, the king of Sind, had sent a convoy of treasure by road. The news came to Anarsing's ears, and he resolved to seize the treasure. He sallied out with his horsemen and attacked the royal guards. But the guards were good men and true, and they resisted so manfully that at last Anarsing's horsemen fled, leaving him a captive in the hands of the king's men. To punish him, the king of Sind took from him his lands, and drove him from the country. The unhappy Anarsing fled to a distant village, where he at last died in poverty and squalor.

On Anarsing's death, his widow gave herself wholly to the care of her son, Ajitsing, and actually worked as a labourer, to support him. At last, worn out by grief and toil, she died when her son had reached the threshold of manhood. Ajitsing, left to his own resources, at first petitioned the king of Sind to give him back his lands, but in vain. Then he thought of Rajbala, his betrothed. He sent a Rajput kinswoman to ask Thakor Partabsing to fulfil his promise and give him his daughter in wedlock.

When the Rajput lady, sent by Ajitsing, reached Veshalpur, Rajbala was sixteen years old and had often thought of the boy to whom she had been betrothed as a child; and when she heard that he had grown up strong, bold, and handsome, she cared little that he had lost everything in the world save a Rajput's honour and a Rajput's sword. So, when Ajitsing's kinswoman came to Veshalpur, the princess sent for her and begged her to tell the prince that she was his, come what might; and that if her father forbade their marriage, she would at least wed no one else.

Thakor Partabsing's answer was different. "I am ready," he told Ajitsing's kinswoman, "to give Rajbala to the prince, but he must prove to me first that he will not be a dependant on her bounty. Let him come with twenty thousand rupees, and he shall have Rajbala for his bride."

The Rajput lady took back the two messages to Ajitsing. He was overjoyed at the words of Rajbala, but he was overwhelmed with misery at the condition made by the old Thakor. So far from owning twenty thousand rupees, he did not own twenty. He remained plunged in grief for some time. Then he remembered a rich Jesalmir banker with whom his father often had dealings. He went to Jesalmir, and, telling the banker his story, asked for the loan of twenty thousand rupees. The old banker looked long at Ajitsing, and at last said, "The twenty thousand rupees are yours, but on one condition. You must promise not to make your wife yours, until you repay my loan with interest." The unhappy Ajitsing thought at first to refuse, but as he could not imagine any other way of getting the money, he at last consented. He took the twenty thousand rupees, and with the money went to Veshalpur.

The old Thakor, who had thought that he had rid himself of Ajitsing, was but little pleased to see him come to his palace with his saddlebags full of money. But, having given his word, he would not go back on it: he married Rajbala to the prince with due ceremonies and gave them one of his palaces to live in.

When the young couple lay down to rest, the prince, to Rajbala's astonishment, drew his sword and put it naked between them. Rajbala was to shy to ask the prince why he acted like this, and several days passed without her doing so. At last taking her courage in both hands, she went up to him and said, "Lord of my soul! I often see that you sigh deeply as if a prey to grief. I beg you, tell me what it is. I am your slave, and aught I can do to help you even to giving you my life—, I will do readily. There is a remedy for every ill; and there is no remedy so good for sorrow, as to tell it to a friend."

At first the prince said nothing. Then he lifted his eyes, and, moved deeply by Rajbala's pure and beautiful face and her simple words, he took her hand in his and told her all his story.

Rajbala, on hearing it, cried, "My lord! You have indeed bought me for a price high above my worth, and I shall always be grateful to you. But you will never get the twenty thousand rupees by staying here. Let us flee away together; I will put on a man's dress, and we will give out that we are brothers-in-law. Let us start at once; for the sooner we start, the sooner we shall be able to pay back that wretched money-lender his twenty thousand rupees."

That very night Rajbala put on a man's dress, and, while all in the palace were asleep, crept with Ajitsing out of the palace. Then they sadled their horses, mounted them, and rode away from Veshalpur.

Some days later the Rana of Udaipur, Jagatsing, was sitting on the roof of his house and looking over his city. Suddenly he saw two young Rajputs riding towards the city-gates. Their faces were new to him; so he at once sent men to bring the strangers to his house. The Rajputs salaamed in the Rana's presence, and, in reply to his questions, the elder said, "We are Rajputs: my name is Ajitsing; my brother-in-law's name is Gulabsing. We went out to seek service, and Heaven has guided us to your court!"

The Rana was pleased with the boy's frank speech. He gave the two youth a home, and ordered that five rupees should be paid them daily. At first Ajitsing and Rajbala were delighted at their reception, but, as time passed, they saw that they were getting no nearer the repayment of the banker's debt. They had reached Udaipur just before the rains began; the rainy season flev y, and Dasara was at hand; yet they had saved nothing out of their daily allowance, which only just sufficed for their food and clothing.

In the meantime Rana Jagatsing had made ready the usual Dasara hunt; and on Dasara day the Rana went out a-hunting, and in his train went Gulabsing and Ajitsing. As they went, a tracker came running up with the news that a lion, as well as some deer, had been marked down. The Rana at once resolved to hunt the lion. "A lion on Dasara day is a fitting quarry indeed," he cried. He mounted an elephant, and rode to the spot with his nobles. The beat began; and the beaters, closing in from three sides, drove the lion through a gap, near which Rana Jagatsing was waiting; the nobles guarded other gaps at various points of the wood. The lion, a huge, maned beast, suddenly charged, roaring, at the Rana's elephant, and so fearful was its appearance that the Rana, panic-stricken, let his bow and arrows fall to the ground. The giant brute sprang on the elephant's trunk, and tore a great mass of flesh out of its forehead. It leapt again to the ground, and then once more sprang on the elephant's head. The elephant, faint with pain and fright, was on the point of falling over, when Gulabsing, calling to Ajitsing that he was going to the Rana's help, rode up with the speed of thought, and pierced the lion with his spear through and through the body. The lion fell to the ground, and, before it could recover itself, Gulabsingh, with a single blow of his sword severed its neck in two. He then alighted and cut off the lion's ears and paws: remounting, he returned at full gallop to his former post.

The Rana, saved by a miracle from death, mounted a fresh elephant, and, calling his nobles round him, asked who it was that had killed the lion; for so swiftly had Gulabsing come and gone, that the Rana had not had time to recognise him. Each time-serving courtier suggested in turn that some friend of his had done the gallant deed; but the Rana shook his head, and, turning his elephant about, set out for his palace. On reaching the palace-door, he bade all his nobles pass in front of him; for he thought that if he saw his rescuer, he would know him again. When Gulabsing passed in front of the Rana, the latter recognised him and called out, "Ho! Rajput! you are he who rescued me and slew the lion!" Gulabsing answered respectfully, "Whomsoever your majesty says slew the lion, slew it." The Rana was puzzled at the answer and was uncertain whether he was right or not. But Ajitsing broke in, "O Protector of the Poor, he who cut off the lion's paws and ears will surely have kept them to prove his deed." The Rana turned angrily on him and said, "Ears or no ears,

paws or no paws, you never killed the lion!" Ajitsing blushed and
said, "No, I did not kill it, but he who did kill it will have its paws
and ears."

Then the Rana remembered that Ajitsing and Gulabsing were
brothers-in-law, and bade the latter, if he could, produce the
brute's paws and ears. Gulabsing leapt from his saddle, pulled
out of his holster the lion's paws and ears, and put them respectfully
at the Rana's feet. The delighted prince praised Gulabsing's
courage and modesty, gave him a robe of honour, and made him
and Ajitsing captains of his guard. Gulabsing he placed in charge
of his state-palace, and Ajitsing he put over his sleeping-apartments.
They could not but accept the royal bounty, but they were both
deeply grieved at their constant separation.

The rains passed and winter succeeded them, but the banker's
twenty thousand rupees seemed as far off as ever. One evening,
about Christmas time, a heavy storm broke. Gulabsing was on
duty at the state-palace, and Ajitsing was with the king. The king
bade Ajitsing go and rest, and went himself to join his queen. At
this time poor Gulabsing, on duty at the state-palace, was feeling
sad and wet and cold. To cheer herself, she sang this quatrain,

"The dark rain pours, the river roars,
    The lightnings flash the storm-gods' ire;
The rain-soaked ground gleams all around,
    And yet, within, my heart's on fire."

Ajitsing heard Gulabsing's song, as he was walking home; its
words struck an echo in his heart, and after a moment's pause
he sang back,

"The Lord is just; in him I trust:
    Heaven watches still though earth be sleeping.

> *Some sin done in some former life*
> *Is now my heart from your heart keeping."*

Gulabsing heard his answer, and murmured with a sigh, "Yes, indeed: it is our destiny and we must bear it."

Now it happened that the Rana's queen was extremely shrewd and clever. When she heard the two quatrains, she said to the king, "Those two captains of your guard are husband and wife. The one on duty over your palace is certainly a woman." The Rana laughed and shook his head: "No, no," he said, "they are brothers-in-law." "Maharaj," said the queen, "you are surely right; still, let us test them and see whether they are brothers-in-law, as you say, or man and wife, as I still think."

The Rana, to please his queen, sent a messenger to call the two Rajputs. When they had come and done obeisance, he eyed them sternly and said, "Gulab and Ajit, tell me at once whether one of you is not a woman." The two were panic-stricken and answered not a word. The Rana asked them still more sternly, "Why do you not answer?" Then, seeing their confusion, he said in a kindlier tone, "Nay, do not fear to tell me your story. Anything that I can, I would willingly do for him who saved my life." Ajitsing then recovered his courage and told their whole story from beginning to end.

The Rana said nothing in reply, but, sending for a slave girl, he bade her take Gulabsing and clothe her in a girl's dress. Next morning he ordered his treasurer to pay Ajitsing twenty thousand rupees, together with the interest due on the debt. The youth had no sooner got the money than he mounted his horse and rode, as hard as he could, to Jesalmir: there he went to the banker and paid him his debt. A year had passed since Ajitsing had borrowed the money, and the old banker had long deemed his money lost;

but he had consoled himself with the thought that he had made much more in former days out of his dealings with Ajitsing's father. So when the money that he thought lost, came back to him, he was the more delighted.

After paying the banker, Ajitsing rode like the wind back to Udaipur, and threw himself at the Rana's feet, to show his gratitude. The king sent for Rajbala and formally bestowed on her the title of "*Pranrakhshak Devi*" or "Life-saving Goddess"; and by this name she became known all through Udaipur. Then he gave her a rich estate and a palace. That very day Ajitsing and Rajbala went to live in it, but this time the prince's sword reposed in its scabbard and no longer lay naked on the couch dividing the sleeping lovers.

Prince Amul Manik
and the Princess Husini

Once upon a time there lived in China a king called Lalu. One day he said to his vizier, Saiphal, "I have no lack of this world's goods, but alas! I have no children." Then he gave his vizier great treasure, and bade him offer it to anyone who could contrive that he should beget a son. The vizier made a proclamation, promising great wealth to anyone who would obtain a son for the king. The proclamation reached the ears of a fakir, who went to the vizier and put a pinch of ashes into his hand, saying, "If only the king gives these ashes in a cup of water to his favourite queen, and she drinks it, God will surely bestow on him a son. He must call the little boy Amul Manik. When Amul Manik grows up, he will possess the thirty-three good qualities. He will become both a wise man and an accomplished rider. When he has finished his education, the king must bring him to me." The vizier promised on the king's behalf that he would do as the fakir said, and he went back to the king with the pinch of ashes.

As the fakir foretold, so it happened. When the boy reached man's estate, the vizier, Saiphal, said, "With your leave, O! king, I will now take the prince to see the fakir." King Lalu agreed, and sent a number of horse-soldiers with the prince, and two horses with jewelled harness and a great treasure of gold and rich raiment as a present to the fakir.

The fakir welcomed the prince; but the same night, at midnight, he roused him; and dressing himself and the prince in disguise, he took the latter to the city of a king, by name Gulasta. After securing a lodging, they explored the whole town, and at last came to the street where the king lived. They looked in at the windows of the palace and saw that it was lit up in the most extraordinary way. The fakir would have led the prince past the palace, but the prince pressed him to stay and look at the blaze of light.

Just then a slave-girl came bearing two ewers, one of gold and one of silver. She said to the prince and the fakir, "Good sirs, who are you, that you stand at this time of night, gazing through the king's windows? You had better go away, or the watchmen will catch you and hale you before the king, and have you punished."

"Lady," answered the fakir, gently, "we have come from a far country and have lost our way. We did not know that this was the royal palace. Pray tell us where there is a mosque, that we may go and rest there."

"Why do you want a mosque?" answered the girl. "Only beggars go there to sleep, while you must be amirs or viziers, or even kings."

The prince interrupted her. "In the name of God, fair lady," he said, "tell me what is the meaning of yonder dazzling light?"

The slave-girl answered, "The light comes from the fairy princess. Husini. She is sitting in her bath; and once she has taken off her clothes, the radiance of her body lights up the whole palace."

The fakir and the prince thanked the slave-girl, and returned to the house, where they had their lodging. As they went, the prince said, "Reverend sir, there is no limit to your wit and wisdom. I implore you to get me married to the fairy princess, Husini," "My son," the fakir replied, "God has already given her to you."

Next morning the prince asked the fakir's leave to return home. On his arrival there, he said to King Lalu, "My father! marry me, I pray you, to the fairy princess, Husini. She lives in a most wonderful palace, and she has no less than sixty slave-girls." Then he went on to describe to the king how, when she bathed, her unrobed beauty lit up the whole of her father's palace. But the king replied, "My son, I wish you to marry your cousin." The prince shook his head impatiently, and said, "I will marry the princes Husini or no one. If you thwart me, I will leave you for ever." The king answered tenderly, "My son, do not be angry without reason. If you love her so much, I will certainly marry you to the princess Husini."

Then the king ordered the vizier Saiphal to go to king Gulasta, and ask for the hand of his daughter, Husini. The vizier went to King Gulasta's city and said to the king, "My lord, King Lalu, my master, asks for the hand of your daughter, Princess Husini, for his son, Prince Amul Manik."

"Good sir, you are welcome," answered King Gulasta; "but my daughter is a grown woman, and I must ask her whether she is willing or not. If she gives her consent, I shall not withhold mine."

King Gulasta went to the princess Husini and told her of Lalu's offer: she replied, "My father, I regard you both as the

Caaba and the Kiblah. I am willing to marry the prince, but on one condition. We must live in separate palaces. If he wants to talk to me, he must say what he wishes to say, to a slave-girl, and she will repeat it to me."

The king told the princess's condition to the vizier, who answered after some little thought, "Very well: I accept on the prince's behalf the princess's terms." For he thought to himself that, once married, the princess would not insist on them. Then he returned to the king and told him everything.

King Lalu asked the prince whether he was willing to abide by the princess's terms. The prince replied, "What can I do? The vizier has already accepted them."

King Lalu thereupon made immense preparations and sent off his son with great state to King Gulasta's country, where he was received with much ceremony and was married to the Princess Husini. After some days of feasting and merriment, the prince took his bride back to his father's city. There, as he had promised, they lived in separate palaces; and whenever the prince and princess had anything to say to each other, they said it to a slave-girl, who carried their messages from one palace to the other.

One day prince Amul Manik went a-hunting, and with his sowars overtook and speared a blue bull. As he was riding home after the hunt, and chatting with his men, he met a fakir, who said to him, "My lord prince, I want to speak with you." The prince mounted the fakir on a camel, and took him to his palace. On their arrival he said, "Reverend sir, what is it that you wish to tell me?"

The fakir made answer, "The princess Husini, whom you have married, is in love with a Dev,† called Suphed. He lives

---

† A kind of genie: a fairy.

beyond the seven seas in a garden called the Bisti garden. Every Thursday the princess Husini gets into a pipal tree with her sixty slave-girls, and by her sorcery makes the pipal tree transport her and her companions to the Bisti garden. I will give you a magic cap, that will make you invisible. Put it on and go to the princess's palace next Thursday evening. You will find her taking her bath. Afterwards she will leave her bath and sit on a carpet, drying her golden hair. Go and sit on the carpet beside her. She will not see you. After drying herself, she will deck herself with costly jewels, scent herself with musk and attar, put bangles on her wrists and anklets on her feet, and clothe herself in rich raiment. Then she will order food, and a meal with be set before her. But before she can touch any of it, eat it all up. She will cry out, "Cook, cook, bring, me my dinner': the cook will answer, 'From what you leave ten or twelve of us usually dine. But to-day, in your joy at the thought of seeing the Dev Suphed, you have gobbled up everything, and now you are asking for more." Husini will feel so ashamed at the cook's retort, that she will say, 'Very well, do not bother: bring me the pipal tree." You should then get up from the carpet and climb into the tree before she does. She will climb into it with her companions, and by her sorcery will make the pipal carry her and then across the seven seas to the Dev Suphed's garden. There you should let them all get down before you, and afterwards follow them. Suphed Dev will welcome them and will take them to his palace, where a hundred other fairies will be dancing. The Dev will say to Husini, 'I will marry you next Thursday, if to-night you will dance instead of the hundred fairies.' The princess will consent, and, putting on a dancing-skirt, will dance before the Dev. When she stops, he will give her a necklace worth nine lacs. Steal it from her and hide it in your belt. She will dance a second time, and the Dev will give her a jewelled robe. Steal that, too, and tie it round your waist. She will dance yet a third time, and the Dev will give her a nose-ring worth another nine lacs. Steal it also, and tie it to your trousers-string. Then go back to the pipal tree, and climb into it. Princess Husini in a short time will say good-bye to the Dev, and with her companions will climb into the tree, which will take you and them back to your own town. There get out of the tree and go to your palace. The princess and her companions will got home and will drink wine, until they fall dead asleep from its fumes. They will sleep late and rise after sunrise. The princess will scold her slaves and will then miss the necklace, the jewelled skirt, and the nose-ring, given her by the Dev. The slave-girls will deny all knowledge of them, and, after protesting their innocence, will advise the princess to go to you, my lord prince. She will agree, and they will all come to your palace. When you see them coming, cover your head with a sheet and begin to snore. The princess will steal up to your bedside, to see it you are really asleep. This will be your chance. Jump suddenly out of bed, catch her, and tear her wings off. She will then be yours always."

Next Thursday prince Amul Manik did just as the fakir had advised him. He put on the invisible cap, and went with the princess Husini on her pipal tree to the Dev's palace and back again.

On the following morning the princess came to the prince's house with all her slave-girls. The prince pretended to snore, and the princess said softly, "There was a time, my prince, when you longed above everything to speak to me. Now, when I come to see you, you lie snoring." The prince was touched by her words and voice, and said, "I was dreaming." "Do, please, tell me your dream," answered the princess. "I dreamt that you had bathed," said the prince, "and that you were drying your golden hair; that, after drying it, you put on rich clothes and jewels; that you then ordered a meal, and I, sitting down besides you, ate it up; that you and I and your slave-girls got into a pipal tree, which rose into the air and carried us into the Bisti garden, where lives Suphed Dev. There Suphed Dev made you dance before him. He gave you a necklace, a jewelled robe, and a nose-ring. All these I took charge of, and am now keeping."

"My prince," said the princess in still gentler tones, "give them all back to me."

"But it was only a dream," laughed the prince. "How can I give them back to you?"

The princess pleaded so hard, and coaxed and wheedled so skilfully, that Amul Manik at last showed her the Dev's presents. Darting forward, she tore them out of his hands, jumped into the air, and vanished.

Then the prince began to lament loudly, "O, why did I not act as the fakir counselled me! He told me she was a fairy. Had I but torn off her wings, she would not have flown away; and she would have been mine always."

The prince fell into so profound a despair that the news of his melancholy state came to the ears of the fakir, who went to him and said, "Did you do as I told you? What happened, when you tore off her wings?" "Nay," said the prince mournfully, "I forgot to tear off her wings, and she flew away. Whatever shall I do now?" The fakir answered, "There is a Samundi‡ horse in your father's stable. Put on it a jewel-studded saddle and bridle: fill the saddle-pockets with diamonds and pearls: take in your

‡ "Samundi" comes from "Samudra". It means a horse that can jump across the sea.

belt money for a three months' voyage: and go in search of Suphed Dev."

The prince did as the fakir told him. He saddled and mounted his father's Samundi horse, and, jumping across the seven seas, rode on until he came to a great forest. In the heart of the forest he saw a lioness that was lame from a big thorn in her foot. When she saw the prince, she called to him, "O, child of man, in the name of Allah! I beseech you to pull out this thorn." "But you will kill me," said the prince, "if I go near you." "Mahomed, the holy prophet, shall be my witness, that I will not hurt you," said the lioness.

The prince thereupon got off his horse, and, calling on Allah to guard him, went up to the lioness and pulled the thorn out of her foot. The lioness roared with the pain, but did not hurt the prince. The sound of her roaring brought to her side her two full-grown cubs. "Child of man," they asked, "are you mad, that you dare come into our very den to hurt our mother?" But the lioness soothed them by telling them that the prince so far from hurting her, has cured her. Then she added, "To reward him for curing me, I give you, my two sons, to him, to be his servants. You must protect him from jhinns, ghosts, fairies, and vampires. You must kill, for his food, deer and antelope. But, above all, you must give your lives, if needs be, to guard him from harm."

The lion-cubs promised to do all their mother told them, and, going to the prince's side, became his servants. As he rode along on his Samundi horse, the lions walked or galloped, one on each side of him.

At last they came to a beautiful lake near which stood a palace: from the palace-door a flight of steps, of gold and silver alternately, led down to the water's edge. The prince said to the two lions, "This must be a fairy's palace." The lions answered, "My lord prince, let us go inside and see."

The prince alighted, tied his horse to a tree, and mounted the steps, one lion in front of him and one behind him. When the prince entered the palace-door, he saw a beautiful girl, dressed like a princess, sitting in an inner room. Suddenly she sprang to her feet and slammed the door in his face. "Open the door," cried the prince. But the girl answered, "Run away! The Dev will be here directly. If he sees you, you are lost." "If you do not open the door," broke in one of the lions, "we will tear it down, plank by plank." "Very well," replied the girl; so saying, she opened the door, came out of the inner room, and seated herself on a couch in the verandah. The prince sat down besides her, and she said, "Well, young lord, what is it you want?" "I want to find the princess Husini. She is my wife, but she had run away from me, and has hidden herself in the country of Suphed Dev." "O, Husini is my sister," said the princess; then, giving him a telescope, she added, "Do you see that pipal tree on the edge of the lake? Well, to-night is Thursday night. Husini will come to-morrow morning with her slave-girls; they will all take their clothes off, and will plunge into the lake. When they are in the water, take Husini's clothes away, and she will be at your mercy."

With these words the princess dismissed the prince. He and the two lions went to the pipal tree at the edge of the lake: and there the lions bade the prince rest, while they watched. Amul Manik lay down and was soon fast asleep.

Early in the morning the whirring of wings woke the prince: "The fairies have come," said the lions. The prince waited until the fairies had all stripped off their robes and had plunged into the water: then he told one of the lions to spring upon Husini's clothes. The lion did so; and the prince, going up to the water's edge, called mockingly to Husini, "You have found your match at last, young lady; this time I shall not let you go in a hurry."

Husini saw that she was at the prince's mercy, for the lions growled fiercely at her, when she tried to go near him and coax him as she had done before. So she said, "I yield, prince: you have beaten me fairly." Then, taking a nose-ring from her nose, she gave it to him, and said, "Next Thursday night come to Suphed Dev's garden. There you will see a number of fairies dressed in scarlet clothes, carrying gold and silver jars. Go up to them and ask for water for your horse. While your horse is drinking, slip this nose-ring into one of the jars. I shall see the nose-ring and take it out. Then I shall send a slave-girl to fetch you. You must come out of your hiding-place, and, when you have reached the middle of the garden, you must call at the top of your voice, "Suphed Dev is going to marry my lawful, wedded wife!" Suphed Dev will then say to you, 'If she is your lawful, wedded wife, you should be able to recognise her. Can you?' You must answer, 'Yes.' Suphed Dev will put a hundred fairies in a row, all exactly like me, and will tell you to pick me out. In the meantime I shall put the nose-ring in my nose, and so you will be able to recognise me."

The prince promised to do what Husini told him, and gave her back her clothes. She put them on and flew away.

Next Thursday the prince did as he had promised. He put the nose-ring in one of the fairies' jars, and the princess, seeing it, sent a slave-girl to fetch him. The slave-girl went to where he was hidden, and called out, "Come, there is going to be a wedding." The prince went with the slave-girl as far as the middle of the garden. Then he called out at the top of his voice, "Suphed Dev is going to marry my lawful, wedded wife." The Dev came forward and said, "If she is your lawful, wedded wife, you should be able to recognise her. Can you?" "Yes," answered the prince. Then the Dev put a hundred fairies in a row, all exactly alike, and on all four sides he posted giant lancers on horseback to prevent the prince escaping. "I will give you three chances," he said. "If you recognise her, well and good: if not, I shall hang you from the walls of my fortress, and the vultures will eat you."

The prince looked up and down the line of fairies. He could not tell one from the other, and not one of them wore a nose-ring. He was on the verge of despair. But the bigger lion-cub whispered to him, "Fear nothing, prince; so long as we are alive, no one shall harm a hair of your head." The Dev gave the prince his second chance, but again he failed to pick out the princess. He said sadly to the lion-cubs, "There is my second chance gone." The lion-cubs whispered back to him, "Courage, prince! You have still one more chance." Then the princess took pity on Amul Manik, and put the nose-ring in her nose. When the Dev told him to try for the third time, the prince saw the nose-ring, and, with a cry of delight, picked out Husini. All the other fairies, glad at his success, clapped their hands with joy, and the Dev said, "Yes, I see the princess is truly your wife; take her." And just as a father gives away his daughter, so he gave Husini to the prince.

Amul Manik stayed for some days as the Dev's guest: then he begged leave to return home. Suphed Dev said very courteously, "So long as you care to stay, prince, you will be welcome; but if you wish to go, go by all means." The prince urged that he must go to his father's kingdom; and with a great train of horsemen and camel-men, and a store of treasure given to him by Suphed Dev, he started with the princess Husini for his father's city.

One night, as they travelled, they halted by a well. The prince and the princess slept together on the same couch: all around them slept the guards. At midnight a Dev, who lived in the well, came out, and, lifting the princess off her couch, as she slept, took her down with him into the well.

Next morning the prince missed Husini. Beside himself with fear and grief, he asked the guards where she was; but they could not tell him. The prince was in utter despair, for he thought that the princess had broken her word and had again left him. But one of the lion-cubs said, "Perhaps she is hiding down in the well. If you tie ropes round us and let us down into the depths, we will see." The guards tied ropes round the two lion-cubs and let them down into the well. When they reached the bottom, they saw a great city stretched in front of them. In the middle of the city was a lovely garden, and in its centre a palace. Looking inside the palace, they saw the Dev, fast asleep, with his head resting on Husini's lap. The princess was delighted, when she saw the lion-cubs, and whispered to them, "Get me out of this dreadful place at once." The cubs lifted the Dev's head ever so gently and put a folded scarf beneath it, so that the princess was able to rise to her feet without the Dev's waking up. Then the lions sprang on the Dev and tore him to pieces.

As they were coming out of the garden, they saw a beautiful Samundi horse, which belonged to the Dev: it was fastened by a golden chain and a padlock to a ring in the wall of the garden. The key was in the padlock, so they unlocked it; and, when they reached the bottom of the well, they had the horse hoisted to the top with themselves and the princess. They told the prince what they had seen, and suggested that he and his guards should go with them once more into the well and carry off the dead Dev's treasure. But the prince refused: "Nay," he said, "my father has no lack of treasure." But he kept the beautiful horse and mounted the princess upon it.

When they reached the shores of the ocean, the two Samundi horses with the prince and the princess, the lion-cubs, and Suphed Dev's gifts upon their backs, sprang right across the seven seas and alighted on the farther coast. There they once more resumed their journey to the prince's own country. When they neared it, and King Lalu heard of their coming, he went out with a great retinue of horsemen and drummers and flute-players and pipers to welcome them, and led Prince Amul Manik and Princess Husini back to his city with great pomp and circumstance. There the prince and the princess lived, no longer in separate palaces, but happily in the same palace, for ever so long afterwards.

Jam Tamachi and Nuri

Once upon a time there ruled over all Sind a Samo prince, named Jam Tamachi. One day, as he sailed in a boat upon the Kanjhar lake, he passed a camp of a fishing tribe, known as Mohanas. Year in, year out, they caught fish, and ate or sold them; and their dirtiness exceeded all imagination. The women were old before their time: they were ugly, and filthy, and covered with skin-disease. They smelt of dead fish and so did everything about them—their baskets, their nets, and their huts. Indeed, if anyone touched their clothes, he would be all day ashamed of himself because of the smell of fish that would follow him everywhere. The children were as dirty as the women, and indeed were scarcely human; for they lived in the water, and swam and dived into the depths of the lake more skilfully even than the otters which lived in the reeds fringing its banks.

But one Mohana girl, called Nuri, was as beautiful as the others were ugly. Her eyes shone like two lamps. Her cheeks were pink as roses; and there was not in all Sind a maid as fair as she was. She was not dirty and evil-smelling like the other fishergirls, but she was as neat and as dainty and as pretty as any princess, and she was as modest and simple as she was beautiful.

It so chanced that Jam Tamachi passed her in his boat, as she stood on the bank. His eyes fell on her, and instantly his heart left his breast, never to return. The fishergirl's eyes had, like a magnet, drawn the king's heart straight out of his bosom.

Jam Tamachi did not delay a moment. He sent for the girl's parents and asked for her hand in marriage. They, poor fisherfolk, were overjoyed at the thought of wedding their daughter Nuri to the greatest king in Sind. And all the fishermen and women throughout Sind rejoiced at the honour done to their tribe by the king's choice.

The king opened wide his treasury, and scattered diamonds and pearls and rubies, and coins of gold and silver, among the fisherfolk as freely as if they had been their own fishes' scales. Then he took Nuri in his arms and made her his queen. But, in spite of all the honour paid her she never became less modest or less simple. To all her flatterers she would answer, "I am but a poor fishergirl. How far above me is the king my husband!" And to the king she would say, "I am a mine of faults. I am nothing compared to your other queens. Still, even though they be far fairer than I, yet love me always, for they do not love you more than I do."

One day Jam Tamachi resolved to test her by comparing her with his other queens. He sent word to all of them that he would go that day for a drive, and he bade them each put on the dress she thought most becoming. He said that, at the end of the drive, he would choose the one he thought fairest, and take her to walk with him. The proud Samo queens put on their gold and jewels and their richest robes, and, with heads high and noses in the air, they drove to the appointed spot. But Nuri dressed herself as a simple fishergirl, in the same dress that she had worn, when she first won the king's heart. No ornament or jewel of any kind glittered on her neck or fingers. Modestly she moved from her carriage towards the king, but her eyes were full of love, as they looked towards him. The other queens turned up their noses higher still at the fishergirl, for they never dreamt that the king would prefer her to any of them. But when Jam Tamachi saw the love that lit up Nuri's eyes and the simple dress in which she had first won his heart, he did not even waste a glance on his Samo queens. Going up to her with outstretched hands, he took her to walk with him, and, after the walk was over, he bade her drive back to the palace by his side. The Samo queens went home weeping tears of rage; but Jam Tamachi cared nothing for their anger. He made Nuri his chief queen, and gave the whole of the Jhanjhar lake as a fief to her kinsmen.

Suhni and Mehar

Once upon a time there lived in Guzrat town, on the banks of the Chenab, a famous potter, named Tallu. His skill in pottery was famed far and wide and had brought him great riches. He had born to him in his old age a lovely daughter. Even as a babe she was so pretty that Tallu gave her the name of Suhni, or the maiden beautiful.

At the same time there lived in Bokhara a rich merchant, called Mirza. For all his riches he was unhappy, because he had no son. One day he heard of a famous fakir, who was reputed to be able to bestow children on the childless. To him Mirza went and implored his help. "Of what use," he cried bitterly, "are all my riches, when I have no son to inherit them?" The fakir pitied the old man, and said, "Your wish shall be fulfilled. You shall be blessed with a son; but beware of the day on which he falls in love!"

Mirza was delighted at the prospect of a son, and paid but little heed to the fakir's warning. He went back home; and in less than a year his wife, although well stricken in years, bore him a son, on exactly the same day as Tallu's wife in Guzrat gave birth to Suhni.

To the little boy Mirza gave the name of Izat Beg. He grew up, and became a skilled musician and a bold huntsman. But one day a traveller from India came to Bokhara, and, meeting Izat Beg, praised to him so warmly the splendours of Delhi and the greatness of the emperor Shah Jahan, that the youth felt that he must see Delhi or die. He asked his father's leave to go, but Mirza would not hear of it.

Izat Beg was so fired with longing to see the city of the mighty emperor, that he could neither eat nor sleep. At last Mirza, fearing for his son's health, gave him leave to go.

Izat Beg set out with a retinue of servants and a great store of money for the journey, and after some weeks he reached Delhi without mishap. There he gave rich presents to several of the courtiers, and in this way obtained an interview with the emperor. Having feasted his eyes on the pomp and state of the court, Izat Beg thought of returning to Bokhara. As he went homewards, he passed, as his ill fortune will it, the village of Guzrat. There he heard of Tallu's fame as a potter and he resolved to buy some of Tallu's earthenware as a present for his father. He sent a servant to Tallu: but the man was so dazzled by the beauty of Suhni, whom he saw in her father's shop, that, without buying anything, he ran back to his master, and cried, "Of the pots I can say nothing, for I had eyes only for the potter's daughter. She is so lovely that she has no earthly rival. No man is fit to wed her save only you, my master."

Izat Beg was so struck by the man's words, that he at once went back with him to Tallu's shop. The moment he saw Suhni, he, too, lost all thought of buying Tallu's pots. All he could do was to gaze, distracted with love, on the potter's daughter. To be the longer with her, he made her show him every pot in Tallu's shop, feigning not to be pleased with any of them. At last Suhni lost all patience with him, and said, "Young sir, if you wish to buy my father's pots, buy them; but if not, pray excuse me, as I have other work waiting for me."

Izat Beg, sooner than displease her, bought all the costliest earthenware she had, and went back to his camp. But he had fallen so deeply in love with Suhni, that he could not bear to leave Guzrat. He opened a shop in the town and stocked it with Tallu's pottery. Each day he went to Tallu's shop and bought pots at any price the potter asked, and, taking them to his ship, sold them for anything the villagers chose to offer him. In this way he soon spent the greater part of his money. His servants, who wished to go back to their homes, began to fear that they would never see Bokhara again. Taking counsel together, they one night robbed their master of such money as he still had, and with it went back to their native country.

Next morning the unhappy Izat Beg woke up to find himself a beggar. For some time he went daily to Tallu's shop and bought pots on credit, promising to pay their price later. But at last Tallu refused to sell him any more and pressed him for payment. Izat Beg pleaded that his servants had robbed him; at the same time he offered to work for Tallu, and so pay off his debt. Tallu agreed, and made him sweep the house daily and fetch clay for his earthenware from the river-bed.

Izat Beg, fearing that he might be sent away, worked so hard that in the end he fell ill. Tallu, taking pity on him, sent him to graze the buffaloes, that he might regain his strength; and as he did not know his real name, he called him Mehar or herdsman.

One day, as Mehar grazed his buffaloes, Suhni came up to him and asked him to give her some milk. Izat Beg consented,

and, as he milked a she-buffalo, he told her his story, how he was
the son of a rich merchant of Bokhara, how he had given up all
his wealth and his home, his parents and his country, all for love
of her. As Suhni heard his tale and saw what a goodly youth he
was, the tears rolled down her cheeks, and before he had done,
she was as much in love with him as he with her.

Every day thereafter Suhni would meet Mehar, and, feigning
to beg milk of him, would pass an hour or more in his company.
At last the village tongues began to wag, and everyone whispered
to his neighbour that Tallu's daughter loved the buffalo-herd. The
talk reached Tallu's ears, and in great wrath he drove Mehar out
of Guzrat. Then, in spite of her tears and entreaties, he married
Suhni to her cousin, who lived close by. But when the wedding
night came, Suhni prayed to Allah to save her from the clutches
of her husband whom she hated; and Allah, taking pity on her,
wrapped him night after night in so deep a sleep that he never
thought of the fair girl by his side.

Now Mehar, driven out of Guzrat, went to live across the
Chenab, so that he might still see by day the roof of the potter's
house, beneath which lived his beloved. He bore their separation
well enough until he heard of her marriage to her cousin. Then,
beside himself with jealousy and grief, he wrote her a bitter letter,
taunting her with her faithlessness to one who had given up all
for her. His cruel words pierced Suhni to the heart. She wrote
back begging him to meet her that night on the river-bank near
her husband's house, and promising that she would show him that
she loved him still.

The letter gave new life to Mehar. That night he swam across
the Chenab, and met Suhni on the river-bank. There, while her
husband slept in the death-like sleep sent him by Allah, Suhni and
Mehar passed many happy hours. They supped off a fish that

Mehar had bought of a fisherman as a present for Suhni, and before the eastern sky grew light, Mehar swam back to his hiding-place across the Chenab.

The next night, and many nights afterwards, he swam the dark water to meet his beloved. Always he brought with him a freshly caught fish, that they might sup together, while her husband slept.

One day, however, there had been a strong wind, and the fishermen had caught no fish. Fearing Suhni might think that he had grown miserly, or that his love for her was waning, Mehar cut a piece of flesh off his thigh, intending to pass it off as a fish that he had bought for her. When he reached the opposite bank, he was so weak with pain that he fainted. Suhni, seeing the blood streaming down his leg, tended his wound. In reply to her questions, he told her what he had done. Tenderly reproaching him, she tied up the wound, and forbade him to swim across the river again. She promised she would swim across to him in future. That night Mehar, wounded though he was, struggled safely back across the river.

Next day Suhni took a seasoned jar from her father's house, and, when night fell, she swam boldly out in to the Chenab with the jar under her. The night was dark and stormy, but the jar bore her up; and with strong, swift stroke she crossed the river, and found Mehar on the bank, ready to clasp her to his bosom. Before morning came, she had swum back and was fast asleep in her husband's house.

Thus, night after night, Sunhi crossed and recrossed the Chenab, borne up by the earthen vessel beneath her. Unhappily, one night, her husband's sister saw Suhni leave her house and, jar in hand, go to the riverside. She followed Suhni, and saw her swim across the river and after some hours swim back again.

Furious for her brother's sake, she vowed that she would rid him of so unfaithful a wife. She noted where Suhni hid her jar, and then went quietly home. But at noon she took an unseasoned pot, and put it in place of the one that had so often carried Suhni across the stream.

When darkness came, Suhni fetched, as she thought the jar that she had hidden, and went to the edge of the river. The rain was pouring in torrents, and the waters roared as if warning her not to go. But trusting in the vessel that had so often carried her, she swam out, as before, into the raging torrent. When she reached midstream, the unseasoned jar crumbled to pieces beneath her, and without its help Suhni could not battle against the current. She struggled bravely for a time, then wearied and sank.

All that night Mehar waited in vain for Suhni on the farther bank. When morning broke, he knew that she must have perished in the cruel water. Life without her, for whom he had given up his home and country, seemed to him worthless. With a great cry to Suhni that he was coming, he sprang into the river and was never seen again.

Hir and Ranjho

Once upon a time a king, named Chuchak, ruled at Jhang Sayal, on the banks of the Chenab river. He had a beautiful daughter, called Hir: her neck was like a swan's, her eyes were like a deer's, and her voice like a coil's. Nor was she only beautiful to look upon: she was also a mine of wit and wisdom. Her father had built her a palace on the banks of the Chenab river, but he did not force her to live in it, as if in a prison. He had a beautiful boat built for her, and in it she would take long trips up and down the river; at night the dwellers on the banks would hear her singing in her cabin, like a nightingale in its cage.

At the same time, in the Hazara country, there ruled four princes, all sons of the same father: of the four the bravest and the most beloved was prince Ranjho. One day there came to Prince Ranjho's palace a traveller. The prince received him courteously and hospitably. Noticing that the traveller was preoccupied and sad, the prince asked him what ailed him. "Nothing ails me, my lord prince," replied the traveller; "but my thoughts are far away in my own city of Jhang Sayal. Over it rules King Chuchak, and there too dwells his daughter Hir, whose beauty I cannot describe, so wonderful it is. If I seem sad and my thoughts wander, it is because I, like all the noble youth of our city, am in love with her. Indeed, it was to gain peace of mind, that I set out on my travels."

The prince's fancy was fired by the tale, and he begged the traveller to describe Princess Hir, however imperfectly. The traveller consented; and so glowing was his tale and so passionate his words, that the prince sprang to his feet. "Promise me that I shall see her," he cried, "or I will kill myself before your eyes." "There is no need to die," said the traveller soothingly; "send an envoy to her father's palace and ask for her hand in marriage."

Prince Ranjho did not send the envoy, for he feared to court a refusal. Nevertheless the image, so deftly painted by the traveller, danced always before his eyes, and he lost all power to eat or sleep. His brothers, seeing his pitiable state, conspired against him, drove him out of the kingdom, and divided his inheritance.

The unhappy Ranjho could think of no better plan than to beg his way to the country of her for love of whom he had lost his kingdom. The way was long from Hazara to Jhang Sayal, and the prince was half dead of fatigue before he came to the Chenab river. At last he saw it in the distance, and on its banks the palace of the princess Hir. Opposite to the palace was moored the princess's boat. The prince called to the boatman, who stood on the deck, "I have come from a far country and I am very weary. Pray, let me rest in yonder boat." The boatman turned, and seeing a tall and gallant youth, guessed him to be of noble birth. Very courteously he answered, "Young lord, that boat is the princess Hir's; I cannot let you go on board."

Prince Ranjho walked towards the boat, hoping to be able to persuade the boatman to let him see the princess. When he reached the water's edge, his worn-out limbs gave way and he fell headlong into the river. The kindly boatman would not let him drown, and, rowing to where the prince was struggling against the current, dragged him into the boat, and let him rest himself in the princess's cabin. A moment later the prince was fast asleep.

It so happened that Hir resolved that day to go sailing on the river earlier than was her wont. With sixty serving maids she walked across the garden that stretched between her palace and the river. When the boatman saw her coming he began to tremble. He called to his wife and said, "Go and appease the princess, or, when she sees this stranger in her cabin, she will have me flayed alive." His wife left the boat and began to scream at the top of her voice. The princess heard her and, running towards her, asked what was the matter. "Oh! Lady, forgive my husband!" sobbed the boatman's wife. "A young man has forced his way into your cabin and is fast asleep on your bed!" When the princess heard these words, her eyes blazed with anger. "How dare he?" she cried. "Where is he? I will kill him." She ran into the cabin, meaning to stab the stranger to the heart, but when, her gaze fell on the sleeping youth, her anger vanished. As she drank in the beauty of the prince, he slowly opened his eyes and, to his surprise, saw before him a maid fairer than the fairies themselves; her eyes were like lotuses, her shape beggared all description. Hir, as if fascinated, came slowly to the side of the cot. The prince held out his arms, and a moment later their lips met.

Hir would not let the prince rise, but, sitting by his side, made him tell her who he was and whence he had come. He told her; and her eyes filled with tears, that he should have lost a kingdom for love of her. Then she said; "Lord of my heart, you cannot stay here in my cabin. Our secret would soon spread abroad. My father would hear of it and would kill you." She thought for some time, and then said, "There is only one way that I can think of, and that is for you to put on a disguise and hire yourself as a buffalo-herd to my father. You can then graze his buffaloes along the river, and I can meet you daily." The prince laughingly consented, and dressed himself as a buffalo-herd in the clothes that Hir procured for him. After bidding him a tender farewell, the princess went to her mother, the queen, and said to her, "Our buffaloes are not thriving. They need a skilled herdsman to look after them. I have seen a herdsman from Hazara, who, so I have heard, has great knowledge of cattle. Let us hire him, and our buffaloes will grow fat." Her mother agreed; and when Ranjho later in the day offered himself for hire, she ordered a thousand buffaloes to be given into his care.

No one was then so happy as the princess. Daily she would slip down the river in her boat, and, meeting Ranjho, would spend the day with him in the shade of some tree on the river's edge.

But, in spite of all her care, her love for Ranjho got noised abroad, and men began to whisper, "The princess Hir has lost her honour to a cowherd!" The rumour at last reached the ears of Hedo, the brother of the queen, and he told his sister. The queen sent for the princess and charged her with her guilt. At first Hir denied the story as mere lying gossip, but at last she told her mother everything. The queen was beside herself with anger, and cried, "Unless you promise to give up this vile cowherd, whom you forsooth dub a prince, I will tell the king, and he will surely put you both to death." Hir shook her head sadly and said, "My mother, I can make no such promise. I have given my life into another's keeping. If I give him up, I give my life up also."

Then the queen rose and brought King Chuchak. When the king heard what his daughter had done, he drew his sword and would have killed her; but, at the queen's entreaty he sent her to prison instead. Then he bade his guards beat Ranjho and drive him from the city.

Half-killed, the unhappy prince dragged himself to a wood at some distance from Jhang Sayal; there he lived, sustained only by the hope that he might again see the princess. Nor did the hope prove vain. The princess pined so in her prison cell, that the queen prevailed on King Chuchak to release her. No sooner was she free, than she made her way to the wood where prince Ranjho was, and fell weeping into his arms. She stayed with him for a short time and then returned to her palace; but every evening she would slip out and take food and drink to Ranjho.

Now Hir's uncle, Hedo, kept a watch on his niece, and, disguised in a beggar's clothes, he followed her to the wood. Returning he told the king what he had seen. King Chuchak, seeing Hir's great love for Ranjho, would have joined them in marriage, but his sons would not hear of it. First they tried to kill prince Ranjho in his lair in the woods; but although he was one to four, he beat them off, until at last they ran away screaming for their lives. Then they formed another plan. They went to the court of King Norang of Norangpur and offered Hir in wedlock to King Norang's son, Khiro. Prince Khiro gladly accepted the princess's hand, and the four princes returned to Jhang Sayal and bade their sister make ready for her marriage. But Hir refused to make any preparations; and when her ladies came to put henna on her, as befitted a bride to be, she drove them out of the room.

The king in despair took his daughter to the kazi. The kazi at first spoke softly to her. "My child," he said, "you should not love a stranger of whom your parents know nothing. You should only love him of whom your parents approve." But Hir would not be cajoled. She stamped her foot and said, "What do you know about love, kazi? If I have drunk the cup of love without my parents' knowledge, I at least know what the cup contains." Then the kazi grew angry and said, "You are a wicked girl; you have committed a great sin. To disobey your parents is to transgress the scriptures." So saying, he took out his holy books, and would have read her passages from them. But Hir stormed at him: "A plague," she cried, "on your scrawls and your zigzags! I do not know a 'zabar'[†] from a 'zer'! What care I if 'alif' stands for Allah or 'mim' for Mahomed or 'ain' for Ali! Your holy books, you say, have come from heaven, but you cannot show me any passage in them that prescribes rules for love: yet love is as old as Adam! Why should a lover need books, when the mirror in his heart shows him the form of his beloved?" The kazi, when he heard this bold reply, foamed at the mouth with rage. "Take her away," he screamed. "Take her away and kill her; she is not fit to live!" The king took her away but he did not kill her. He sent her to Norangpur, where, sore against her will, she was married to prince Khiro.

In the meantime Prince Ranjho donned the garb of a fakir, and went on foot to Norangpur. Passing close to Hir's window he contrived, with the help of her sister-in-law Sahti, to make his presence in the town known to her. The same day Hir cried out that a cobra had bitten her in the foot; and, falling on the ground, she feigned to be in agony. The court-doctors were sent for, but they could do nothing. At last Sahti suggested that the fakir who had just come to Norangpur, might perhaps effect a cure. The fakir was sent for, and at once promised to cure the princess,

---

† "Zabar" is the sign for the vowel 'a' and 'zer' the sign for the vowel 'i'.

provided that he and she were left alone together. The others left them, and Hir and Ranjho embraced. Hir promised her lover to leave the palace and run away with him that very night. Then, to soothe the suspicions of her companions, he began to recite "mantras" loudly enough for those outside to hear. In a short time he went out of the room and pronounced the princess cured; and, calling in her companions, he claimed, and received a rich reward.

That night the princess slipped unseen out of the palace; and, joining Ranjho outside the walls of Norangpur, she fled with him towards Hazara. In vain King Norang sent horsemen to catch them; for, thinking that the fugitives must be fleeing to Jhang Sayal, the horsemen took the wrong road and so never came up with them.

After great toil and hardships, Ranjho and Hir reached Hazara. There Ranjho's brothers had ruled so ill and harshly, that when the people saw their favourite prince again, they rose in thousands, and, putting the prince at their head, stormed the palace and drove his three brothers from Hazara, just as formerly they themselves had driven out the prince. In this way Ranjho became master of his father's entire kingdom. He married the Princess Hir and made her his queen, and together they ruled over the people of Hazara for many years afterwards.

Birsing and Sunderbai

Once upon a time there ruled in Sayla, a king, called Kesarising. He had a daughter, by name Sunderbai, who was her father's choicest treasure: for not only did she know the Sanskrit tongue and all the shastras[†] and the sciences of the time, but she was brave, resolute, and generous; while in beauty she had no equal among the maids of India. Thus she fully deserved, in every sense, the name of Sunderbai or the beautiful maiden.

In spite of all her learning, Sunderbai was as light-hearted as any of her companions. One day she was playing with her girl friends in one of her father's gardens. The garden was filled with great shady trees and with rare sweet-scented flowers: in the middle was a palace, provided with all the comfort and luxury of which the times knew. Sunderbai and the maidens with her had passed the heat of the day in the shelter of the palace, and had just felt it to play in the garden.

[†] Learned books.

Now it so happened that at this time the crown prince of Valabhipura, Birsing, reached this spot. He had been hunting and had lost his companions. Weary with the heat, he had come to rest beneath the trees in King Kesarising's garden. Choosing the shadiest spot, he spread his saddlecloth on the ground, and lay down upon it. Suddenly he heard voices singing close by. Forgetting his fatigue, he rose to his feet, and began to walk towards the sound, thinking to join the singers, whoever they might be. As he walked, he peered through the bushes, and suddenly he saw that the singers were a party of girls. He stopped; and, thinking it unbecoming to go further, he sat down behind a tree and listened to the song.

When it was over, the girls began to talk together. Suddenly one said, "When I marry, I shall lead my husband a life of it! Men trample on their wives, just as if they were their boots; and yet, if a man has no wife, he is perfectly useless." The princess answered, "Yes, indeed! But I am going to marry Prince Birsing, the son of the king of Valabhipura; and I mean so to win his love that he will have no eyes for any other. If he does not treat me as I mean him to, I shall show him by my strength and courage that women are every bit as brave as men. He will then be so ashamed of himself, that he will love and honour me, and will do whatever I want him to." A third girl said, "But, princess, you surely do not mean that your husband will never take a second wife?'

Birsing was all attention on hearing his name. He realised that the second speaker must be Kesarising's daughter, and that it was impossible for him to stay where he was any longer. He turned to leave the garden, but, before he went, he looked through the trees at Sunderbai. Her face was bright as a summer moon, and her form was fashioned in the most perfect mould.

Thoughtfully the prince replaced his saddle, and left the garden, leading his horse. Meeting some men outside, he asked whether the princess lived there. They told him the garden belonged to Sunderbai. Thereupon Birsing vowed that he would make Sunderbai his bride.

When the prince had ridden home, he told the king, his father, that he wanted to marry Kesarising's daughter. As the two families of Valabhipura and Sayla were equal in rank, Birsing's father sent a priest to Kesarising, to call for Sunderbai's hand for his son. Kesarising readily agreed to the betrothal; the wedding was celebrated with great splendour, and Sunderbai was borne in state to Birsing's palace.

The young prince wished to see whether Sunderbai would make good her boast; so, on their marriage night, he did not go near her. The princess wondered at his conduct, and her slave-girls and companions wondered still more; but Sunderbai bravely hid her feelings, and on her lovely face could be seen no sign of grief or anger.

After some months had passed, one of the princess's maids came and said to her, "Princess! to-day is New Year's day, and there is a great festival at the temple. Would you not like to go and see it? It will cheer you?" Sunderbai agreed, and at once made ready to go.

Early in the morning the princess left her palace in great state, and went with her maids and ladies to the temple. There every precaution had been taken that, while the princess was inside, no male should enter. But when Birsing heard that Sunderbai had gone to the temple, he also went there with some of his courtiers, unseen by her, so that he might discover what she would do. None could refuse Birsing admittance; so he followed Sunderbai to where she was worshipping Parvati. As she worshipped, she prayed aloud, "Queen of the world, bless in all ways my husband!" Then she raised her head, and, as she did so, her eyes met those of Birsing, who at this moment came out of his hiding-place, and said with a mocking smile, "Is this the way you mean to conquer your husband by your strength and valour, as you boasted in your garden?"

Sunderbai then knew that Birsing had overheard her. Clasping her hands, she answered, "Lord of my life, women are but foolish creatures. A girl's chatter is of no account. Pay no heed to mine and in your wisdom forgive me!" But Birsing shook his head, and answered sternly, "Until you make good your words, princess, I will not enter the door of your palace." So saying, he turned on his heel and left the temple.

For some moments Sunderbai stood looking after him, the picture of distress; then, thinking that if she wanted to win him, she would have to give him proofs of her courage and strength, she finished her worship and left the temple.

For many days and nights Sunderbai pondered what she should do, but she could think of nothing. At last, she resolved to flee from the palace. Outside, Parvati might send her the chance which she sought. But to quit the palace and slip through the guards, was no light thing. At length she took from her finger a ring, given her by her father, Kesarising; handing it to a slave-girl, she said, "Take this to the king, my father, and say, "The jewel in the ring is loose. Please get it put right.' The slave-girl reached Sayla safely, and gave the king Sunderbai's ring and message.

When Kesarising saw the ring, he guessed that some calamity had overtaken his daughter. He dismissed the slave-girl with a present; and, when alone, he took out the stone. Underneath was a note, on which was written, "My father, when two parrots quarrel, it is useless to keep them in the same cage. One day in the garden I said to one of my companions that if I married Birsing, I would by my strength and valour make him madly in love with me. The prince overheard what I said, and is putting me to the proof. I am in great trouble. Send me, I pray you, a man's dress, a coat of mail and a swift horse: but let no one know."

King Kesarising was greatly troubled by the letter. "A man's dress, a coat of mail, and a swift horse," he said to himself, "are easily sent: but how can I send them without letting others know?" After much thought he resolved secretly to dig a tunnel from a mountain near Valabhipura into his daughter's palace. At great cost and immense labour he made the tunnel, and conveyed the horse, the armour, and the dress to his daughter. Sunderbai was delighted, and, donning the dress and the coat of mail, warned her maids and ladies to tell no one of her flight. Then, mounting on her horse, she rode out through the tunnel.

Two days later a bold and handsome youth came to Valabhipura, and asked for an audience with the king. It was granted; and all the court marvelled at the stature and beauty of the stranger. The king, wondering, asked him, "What is your name and who is your father?" "My name is Ratansing," was the reply. "My father is a Rajput, but I have quarrelled with him, and I have come here in search of service. I have sworn an oath not to reveal my father's name or country. Any work you give me, I will do. Give me but a chance of proving my skill and courage, and you will never regret it."

The king liked the bold words and fearless bearing of the young Rajput, and made him at once take his place among his nobles. Ratansing salaamed, as if deeply grateful. Although he had no chance of showing his mettle in the battlefield, he soon proved it in the chase, where by his skill in horsemanship and bold riding he always out-distanced the other nobles. On this account Birsing

conceived the greatest affection for Ratansing; and, never
suspecting who the new-comer was, he told him in the strictest
confidence all about Sunderbai's pride and arrogance, and how
he had treated her as she deserved. Ratansing laughed and said,
"You are not treating her over-well, are you, prince?" Birsing
replied, "I really love her better than anyone else in the world;
nor do I wish ever to marry anyone else. But I want to test her
and see if she will make good her boast. If she is a true Rajputni,
she will do so." Ratansing smiled but said nothing.

Some days afterwards it so happened that a fierce lion began
to haunt the outskirts of Valabhipura. Every day it killed and ate
one, if not two, of the inhabitants. The young nobles tried every
means to destroy it, but none succeeded.

At last the outcry was so great that the Rana ordered Ratansing
to hunt it. Ratansing joyfully accepted the task, and asked that
the king's artificers should make him a hollow iron image of a
man. He had the image put in a spot where the lion had killed
several men, got inside it, and sent away the men who had
brought it. At midnight the lion came, and, thinking the image
to be a man, rushed at it. As it tried in vain to knock the image
over, Ratansing slipped out, and with a single blow of his sword
cut the lion's head off. Then he dragged the carcase home, and,
thrusting it beneath his cot, went to sleep.

Birsing, who had all that night been consumed with fears for
his friend, went early next morning to Ratansing's home, to learn
the news. The latter would not receive Birsing in his room, lest
he should pierce his disguise. He went to the door to greet
Birsing, dragging the lion's carcase after him. Birsing was delighted
to see it, and, taking Ratansing with him, went off at once to tell
the news to the king, who bestowed on Ratansing a robe of
honour and a grant of land.

A year or so later the king went a-hunting in a distant forest, taking with him Ratansing. A neighbouring king heard through his spies of the king's absence, and, making a sudden onslaught, took Valabhipura. Now, through illness, Birsing had not gone with his father to the hunt; so he too fell into the enemy's hands. Having taken the capital and the heir apparent, the neighbouring king set up defences round Valabhipura, so as to make it impregnable.

When the news reached he king he was broken-hearted. "My son! O my son Birsing!" he cried in Ratansing's hearing. "If they kill you, how can I live without you? Had I but you with me, I should soon recover my city."

Ratansing comforted the old king as best he could, and then he obtained leave to go to Sayla and bring what troops he could from Kesarising, the king of that place, whom Ratansing said was his kinsman.

Ratansing rode swiftly to Sayla, told Kesarising all that had happened, and, begging from him a picked body of lancers, returned to the old king's camp. He led his force to the place where Kesarising had, at Sunderbai's instance, dug a tunnel into Valabhipura. There he divided his men into four squadrons of fifty each. He bade three of them make feigned attacks on different parts of the city, while he himself with the fourth squadron entered the city through the tunnel. The foemen inside easily repulsed the attacks, but while they were rejoicing at their easy victory, Ratansing entered the city through the tunnel, took the garrison by surprise, and, after killing many of them, opened the gates for the three squadrons outside, and with them completed the capture of the city. Ratansing then freed Birsing from the loathsome dungeon in which he had been confined, and, after embracing his friend, took him to his father. Both Birsing and his father poured out their thanks, but Ratansing answered modestly that he was but a soldier in the service of Valabhipura, and that he had only done his duty.

Shortly afterwards Ratansing excused himself, pleading that he had to entertain some friends who had just come from his old home to see him. Taking leave of the king, he went into the fort. As he did not return, Birsing began to look for him; but he could find him nowhere. At last some men told him that they had seen him going to Sunderbai's palace.

Instantly a dark suspicion entered Birsing's mind. "Ratansing," he said to himself, "must be my wife's lover. That is how he learnt about the secret entrance to the city. Through it he must have gone in old days, to have stolen meetings with her." Drawing his sword, he rushed up the steps that led to Sunderbai's chamber. She was alone, and rose to greet him: but her humility only added fuel to his anger. "Where is your Ratan, you faithless woman?" he cried. Sunderbai, amazed at the question, answered, "Lord of my soul, of whom do you speak?" Birsing's fury grew fiercer still. "Vile wretch!" he roared. "You know well of whom I speak. Where is Ratan, your lover, he who used to visit you by the secret passage into the city? Show him to me at once, sorceress, that I may cut off his head, and then stab you to the heart." Sunderbai drew herself to her full height, and said, "What better death could I wish, sweet lord, than death at your hands? But before you stab me, look well into my face: perchance you may find there your friend, Ratan, with whom you are now so angry."

Birsing looked into Sunderbai's face, which now smilingly mocked him. At once he recognised her as the Ratansing whom he sought, the Ratansing who had saved his father's throne and his own life. Falling at her feet, he implored her pardon. But Sunderbai continued to tease him. "Confess, dear lord," she said, "that I have redeemed the pledge I made in my father's garden, and that women can be every bit as brave as men."

Birsing embraced her tenderly, and, knowing that she was right, begged again—and this time obtained—her forgiveness. Taking her by the hand he led her back to his father's presence, and there made her tell the whole story of her adventures from beginning to end.

From that day on, Birsing no longer neglected Sunderbai, but was her devoted lover, and until the hour of her death he never thought of wedding any wife but her.

Kamsen and Kamrup

Once upon a time there ruled in Magrur town a great king named Narkarpal, who with his vizier Nazarsaf held sway over all Sind. The king had a son, Kamsen, whose face was so beautiful, that when he wandered through the forests with his companions, even the wild beasts fell in love with his beauty.

One summer night a band of fairies flew over Kamsen, as he slept on the roof of his palace, and, seeing the handsome boy, said, one to the other, "Never have we seen so fair a youth." Then they flew back to their own moonlit gardens, heavy with the scent of musk and the perfume of flowers. There they met another band of fairies, and told them of Kamsen's beauty. The other fairies clapped their hands with joy and said, "We flew over Guzarat, and we saw a maid, fairer than any one of us, sleeping on a place there. Let us put her cot and this youth's side by side to-morrow night."

When the next night came, the fairies took Kamsen's cot from Magrur; and, bearing it in the twinkling of an eye to

Guzarat, they put it beside Kamrup's. Then they woke the prince and princess, who at once fell in love with each other and spent the night talking together. At dawn they fell asleep; and the fairies came, and, lifting the prince's cot, put it back on the roof of his palace in Magrur.

When the prince rose that morning he was distraught with love for Kamrup, and day by day he faded for want of her, like a flower for want of water. At last the king bade the prince's companions learn from him what ill had befallen him. They plied Kamsen with questions. At last the prince said, "I awoke one night to find my cot beside that of a princess more beautiful than any daughter of earth. Then, when dawn came and I fell asleep, my cot returned to my own place." "But where does the maid live?" asked his companions, "and what is her name?" "Her name is Kamrup," said the prince, for the princess had told him. "But I do not know where she lives."

Kamsen's companions repeated his words to the king, who bade the vizier set forth with five hundred men, to look for Kamrup. Their trappings and tents were gay with gold and jewels, and they wandered southwards for five months until they came to Guzarat. There the vizier sent for a villager, and asked him who the king of the land was. "His name is Jaysingrai," answered the man. "He is a great king, and has a mighty army and a boundless treasure. Yet of all his possessions the most wonderful is this lovely daughter, Kamrup. But of late some evil has come to her; for she no longer has any joy of life, but sits alone, murmuring the word Kamsen. Then Nazarsaf knew that he had reached his goal, and he bade his men pitch their tents.

King Jaysingrai was a Jadeja Rajput; and, when he heard that a band of foreigners had camped outside his city, he sent for the vizier, and asked him why and whence he had come. "My lord king," replied Nazarsaf, "I come from Narkarpal of Magrur, the greatest king in all Sind. He has bidden me ask the hand of the Princess Kamrup for his son, Kamsen, who is the fairest of the children of men."

King Jaysingrai asked the vizier many questions about Magrur and King Narkarpal, and approved the answers. Then, after consulting his nobles, he gave the vizier a cocoanut, to take back to Magrur as a token of acceptance, and bade him ask the king to bring the prince within twelve months, that he might wed the Princess Kamrup.

When the vizier returned to Magrur, the king rejoiced greatly and held high revel in the city. When the appointed time came, he set out with the prince, entrusting his town to the vizier's care. He took a great store of presents for the princess and the king, and many elephants with rich howdahs, and horses with gay trappings. Unhappily he had only gone a day's march from Magrur, when an army of his enemies ambushed and slew him and many of the nobles with him. The prince with the rest fled back to Magrur, to which his enemies at once laid siege. But the prince defended his town bravely, and sent a messenger, to tell King Jaysingrai of the death of his father and of his own troubles.

When King Jaysingrai read the letter, he grieved greatly, but in no long time he had sorrows of his own. A neighbouring king, who desired Kamrup's beauty, invaded Guzarat, and, besieging King Jaysingrai's city, forced him to promise him Kamrup as the price of peace.

But Kamrup had loved the prince ever since the night that the fairies had put their cots side by side; so, when she heard that her father had betrothed her to his enemy, she wept night and day, until she could bear it no longer. Then she wrote a letter to Kamsen and sent it by a messenger, begging him to come and claim her.

The messenger, disguised as a fakir, came to the enemy's lines that surrounded Magrur. Passing through the lines at night, he came to a loop-hole in the fortress-walls, and whispered to the sentry that he had a letter for the prince. The sentry told Kamsen, who came to the loop-hole, took the letter, and, when he had read it, wrote in answer that he would surely claim Kamrup, if only she would wait for him. This letter he gave to the messenger, who made his way back to Guzarat and gave it to the princess.

In the meantime the prince's enemies tried daily to take Magrur, but in vain. At last, weary of the siege, they struck their camp, and returned to their own country. Then the nobles of Magrur placed the prince on the throne of his father and hailed him as king over all Sind.

But in spite of his enemies' defeat and his own succession, Kamsen's thoughts turned ever to the princess; and, calling round him his nobles, he told them that he must go to Guzarat and claim Kamrup. Then nobles answered that it was now too late, and that the king, to whom she was betrothed, guarded all the approaches of her palace. But Kamsen still said that he must go.

Then Nazarsaf spoke. "My lord king," he said, "do not go yourself; send a slave girl, and she will devise some scheme, if possible." The king agreed, and choosing a pretty slave-girl, Dilharan by name, sent her to Guzarat.

The slave-girl, who was as wise as she was pretty, dressed herself as a female doctor, and gave out that she could cure all ills by her remedies and her charms. She also scattered money in charity broadcast, so that the fame of her coming went before her to Guzarat.

When the new doctor reached the city, Kamrup at once sent for her. But the slave-girl affected to give herself airs, and said haughtily to the princess's messenger that she was not at the beck and call of kings or queens. Then Kamrup sent a palki to fetch her. When the doctor reached the palace, Kamrup put her scarf round the slave-girl's neck by way of entreaty and begged her to cure her of her illness.

The slave-girl looked very wise, and, opening her holy books, feigned to read in them. "One night," she said, "so I see in my books, you woke to find by your side a cot and in the cot a beautiful youth." The princess at once guessed that the doctor was but an envoy of her lover, and questioned her. The slave-girl laughingly replied that she had come from Kamsen and that he was just as ill as Kamrup was, and of the same sickness. Then the princess said, "The day of my marriage with my father's enemy is drawing near. Unless Kamsen comes soon to claim me, it will be too late. Go back to him and tell him to wait for me in a wood outside the town and to the east of the road from Magrur."

The slave-girl went back to Magrur with all speed, and told the king what Kamrup had said. At once Kamsen entrusted his kingdom to Nazarsaf, mounted the swiftest horse in Sind, and rode as fast as he could to Guzarat. When he came near Jaysingrai's city, Kamsen searched until he found the wood wherein he was to meet the princess. Then he went to the house of a neighbouring farmer, said that he was a rich merchant, and asked if he might lodge there for a few days. At the same time he gave the farmer a hundred gold pieces. The farmer gladly welcomed so generous a guest, and with his help Kamsen sent word secretly to the princess that he had come to claim her.

When Kamrup got Kamsen's message, she gave out that she would go on a pilgrimage towards the wood, where, as she knew, her lover was awaiting her. When Kamrup and her companions reached the wood, the princess entered it, as if to worship a hollow tree. Her love saw her coming, and, lifting her on to his horse, galloped off with her as fast as he could. Kamrup's companions waited for her, and then searched and called for her in vain. Then they said one to another, "Some god must have fallen in love with her and carried her off." And they went back and told King Jaysingrai that a huge bird had swooped down from the sky and had carried off the princess.

In the meantime Kamsen, with Kamrup in his arms, rode all day; to baffle pursuit, he left the road, and rode across the open country. As evening fell, he saw a house and smoke rising from it. Now in the house lived an old man who has married a witch and by her had seven "rakshas"† sons. When Kamsen entered the house with Kamrup, the old man welcomed them and invited them to stay the night. But the witch fell in love with Kamsen's beauty and plotted to kill Kamrup, while she and her husband slept. That night she went softly to where the lovers were sleeping, hoping to surprise Kamrup. But the princess was watching over her lover, bow in hand. The witch snarled with rage, when she saw Kamrup awake. Kamrup fitted an arrow to her bow, and instantly the witch rose high into the air with the noise of a cannon-shot. Then she turned herself into a great hill and advanced to crush Kamrup. But the princess feared nothing, and, drawing her bow, shot two arrows into the centre of the hill. They pierced the witch's heart; and, resuming her proper shape, she fell dying on the ground.

King Kamsen awoke and the princess told him what had happened. "My lord," she said, "let us leave this dreadful place lest other demons attack us."

Together they left the house; and Kamsen, giving Kamrup his hand, lifted her on to his horse, and sprang up in front of her.

---

† Giant.

He had hardly done so, when the princess saw the witch's seven rakshas sons rushing after them. The witch had lied to Kamrup, telling her that her seven sons had all been killed by robbers. But now they were running after the king and Kamrup, at each stride covering a furlong. The king spurred his horse, vainly trying to leave them behind, but the rakshas soon caught them up. Then the princess, fitting an arrow to her bow, shot down the leading rakshas and, after him, five others. The seventh took fright and ran away.

The king and the princess continued their flight until they came to a lovely lake, shaded with trees and covered with lotuses. On the bank of the lake they saw a man who seemed sick unto death. The king asked him who he was, and the man replied, "I came from heart; but on the way I fell ill, and my companion left me by this lake." The king's heart softened towards the stranger; he gave him food and bade him stay with him as his servant. Then the king went to bathe in the lake; he took off his clothes, and gave them and his bow and arrows into his new servant's charge. But when the king was waist-deep in the water, the servant, who was really the seventh son of the witch, took up the king's bow and arrows, and shot him through the heart. The king fell forward, and the waters closed over him. Then the wicked rakshas dressed himself in the king's clothes, and went back to Kamsen. He told her that he had killed her lover and that now she must be his bride.

The princess saw that she could only escape from the wretch's power by guile; so she feigned assent, but bade him go and bathe in the lake, and then return to her. The rakshas fell into the brave princess's snare, and, taking off his clothes, plunged into the lake. Then Kamrup, coming up behind him, shot him down, just as he had shot her husband. He also fell forward, and the waters closed over him. Kamrup next slipped off her dress, and, diving into the lake, brought her husband's body to the surface. She dragged him ashore, and, putting his head in her lap, began to mourn aloud. All that day she mourned for him. At midnight, overcome with sorrow, she took her dagger in her hand and was about to plunge it into her heart.

Now it so chanced that Mahadev‡ saw Kamrup from his heaven, Kailas, and, pitying her, descended with Parvati to earth. He asked Kamrup why she mourned, and she told him her story. Then the great God, seeing Kamrup's love for the dead king, restored him to life. He rose, rubbing his eyes, as if he had been aroused from sleep; and, as he and Kamrup embraced each other, Mahadev and Parvati reascended to heaven.

The same day Kamsen and Kamrup once more mounted their horse, and rode, as they thought, towards Magrur. On the sixteenth day they saw a great city in front of them. Riding to the nearest gate, they learnt that it was Deval, the city of Raja Kand. When the Raja heard that a strange youth with a beautiful girl had come to the city, he sent for Kamsen, and asked him who he was and whence he come. "I am Kamsen, the son of Narkarpal, king of Magrur," replied the young king proudly. "I was hunting a wild boar, but I lost my way and at last I have come here. The rajah welcomed Kamsen, gave him rich clothes, and bade him stay in his city, Deval.

A few days later a farmer came to Raja Kand crying out that a lion had fallen on his flocks, and called on Raja Kand to kill it. Kamsen stepped forth and said, "My lord king, let me repay your kindness by killing the lion. Raja Kand assented, and Kamsen went back with the farmer to his homestead. There they saw

---

‡ Mahadev is another name for the Hindu God, Siva: Parvati is his wife.

the lion devouring a cow. When Kamsen approached, the lion rushed at him; but Kamsen drove his spear into its heart, as it charged, and killed it. Then he returned to Raja Kand, who was so pleased with him that he gave him the hand of his daughter, the princess Waso.

Now the princess Waso was a wicked sorceress, who had killed all her previous suitors. When she learnt that her hand had been given to Kamsen, she tempted him to come to her palace; and there by her spells she turned him into a sheep and tied him up in the courtyard.

For some days Kamrup missed her lover, the king: then she went to search for him. She looked for him all through the town, and, seeing his footprints, she tracked him to Waso's palace. Then she sent home, and disguising herself as a young man,, went past Waso's window. Waso saw, as she thought, a beautiful youth, and straightway beckoned to him to enter her palace. Kamrup did so, but the moment she entered Waso's room, she seized the wicked sorceress, and, throwing her on her bed, tied her hand and foot, and threatened to kill her, unless she freed Kamsen from her spell. Waso screamed and, hearing her cries, Raja Kand rushed in. Then Kamrup told him all Waso's wickedness. Raja Kand begged her to forgive the princess, but she would not free Waso, until the sorceress had restored Kamsen to his human form and until she herself had cut off Waso's long hair, thus robbing her of her magic power.

Not many days afterwards King Kamsen was married to Waso with great pomp and circumstance; and for many days he feasted and hunted in honour of his wedding. But hatred of Kamrup burnt as fiercely as even in the heart of Waso. One day she saw the beautiful princess bathing; and the sight of her unveiled beauty added such fuel to her hatred that she vowed to destroy her. Robbed of her hair, she could not practise her wicked magic; nevertheless she laid a deep plot to compass Kamrup's ruin.

That evening when Kamsen came to Waso's chamber, she would not speak to him. At last, in answer to his repeated questions she said: "That beautiful girl, whom you brought with you, has a heart as bad as her face is fair. She is daily unfaithful to you." King Kamsen answered angrily, "There is no woman on earth as pure as she is. Twice she has saved my life; she would never be unfaithful to me." But Waso said, "Lord King, so you think; but instead of going to the hunt to-morrow, watch her palace, and you will see one of her lovers climb in at her window." King Kamsen agreed to watch Kamrup's palace, for he felt sure that the tale was utterly false.

Next day Kamsen mounted his horse as if to go a-hunting, and then returned to a spot from which he could see Kamrup's palace. After the king had gone, the wicked sorceress, Waso, dressed herself like a man: then, going to Kamrup's palace she climbed with great skill up to her window. King Kamsen saw her; and, thinking Waso to be Kamrup's lover, he did not stay to see more, but galloped homewards and bade his executioners seize Kamrup. "Take her into the desert," he cried, mad with grief and jealousy, "and tear her eyes out!"

The executioners seized the unhappy princess, and took her to a barren plain outside the city. But there they had pity on her youth and beauty and let her go. Then they caught and killed a deer: taking out its eyes, they carried them back to Deval, and showed them to the king.

The poor princess walked all that day until she could walk no longer. Then she sat down and wept bitterly. Suddenly she thought of the fairies, who had first brought her and Kamsen together, and prayed to them to help her. Instantly a great band of fairies stood beside her. She told her story; and they, pitying her, bore her away to their heavenly dwelling place, to live with them. They gave her a fairy serving-maid to wait on her, and a beautiful fairy house to live in, with a lovely fairy garden round it, in which she might wander and forget her grief among the perfume of its fairy flowers.

In the meantime Kamsen, convinced of Kamrup's guilt, fell a victim to the wiles and charms of the princess Waso. For a long time he forgot all about Kamrup, and daily fell deeper in love with the false beauty of Raja Kand's daughter. But one night he woke from his sleep and began to think about Kamrup. He remembered how cruel he had been, and what little proof he had had of her guilt. At last in a fury of passion he drove his dagger deep into the heart of the sleeping witch at his side, and then rushed madly out of the palace, through the town, and into the barren plain beyond. Flinging aside his rich dress, he became a half-naked anchorite.

For many days Kamsen roamed about the endless waste. At last he came to a wood by a little lake, where he sat down under a tree, to rest for a space. Now it so chanced that a pair of birds were sitting in the branches of this very tree, and one began to talk to the other. Said one: "That man whom you see below us, is dying for love; yet he himself ordered her, whom he loved, to suffer a cruel death." Said the other: "Pray tell me his story." The first bird told how Kamsen had sentenced Kamrup, although guiltless, to death, and how the fairies had carried her away. Then the bird said, "Yet there is a way by which, if he knew it, he could win her back. He should sit over a fire for eight days, fasting and inhaling smoke. On the eighth day the fairies, with their queen, Shapuri, and Kamrup, will come and bathe. He should then seize queen Shapuri's robes and refuse to give them back, unless she restores Kamrup to him."

Kamsen heard with mingled sorrow and joy what the birds said. For eight days he sat over a fire, fasting and inhaling smoke. On the eighth day, as the bird had foretold, the fairies, with their queen, Shapuri, and Kamrup, came to bathe in the lake. King Kamsen waited until all the fairies had taken off their dresses and had plunged into the water: then, creeping out of the wood unperceived, he took queen Shapuri's robes, and stole back with them to his hiding place. After a time the fairies came out of the water, and each one put on her dress. But Queen Shapuri's robe was nowhere to be seen. She searched for it in vain along the bank of the lake. Then she entered the wood, and saw Kamsen with her dress held firmly in his arms. Flaming with anger, she bade him give her back her robe: but Kamsen demanded that she should give him Kamrup in exchange. The angry fairy queen grew until she became a giantess; then she changed into an elephant, and threatened to trample Kamsen underfoot. But the king smiled sadly at her, and said, "Life with Kamrup is precious to me: but without her I would welcome death gladly." At last pity took the place of anger in queen Shapuri's heart. Kamrup, seeing this, joined her entreaties to Kamsen's. "Give me back to him," she pleaded: "you first united us; do not part us now." Then the queen gave way, and, restoring Kamrup to Kamsen, took her robe in exchange.

At the fairy queen's bidding, the fairies lifted the two lovers high in the heavens and bore them back to Sind, until in the distance they could see the turrets of the king's own city, Magrur. Then they put them down on earth. "This is your kingdom, Kamsen," said queen Shapuri; "but a false king has won over your army and has seated himself on your throne." With these words the fairies vanished.

The king sighed deeply when he heard these tidings from the fairy queen: but taking, courage, he said, "A little to the north of Magrur is a palace. I see no tracks of anyone going that way. Let us go there, and take counsel what we shall do." The two lovers reached the empty palace at midnight, and there they spent the night, happy at being reunited, but full of cares for the future.

Next morning the king, looking from the window of the palace, saw an old woman who had nursed him in his childhood. He called to her, and she greeted him with loud cries of welcome and tears of joy. Then she asked him where he had been and why he had stayed away so long. The king told her all his adventures and how at last the fairies had brought him and Kamrup back to his own city. Then he made her tell him what had happened in his absence, and who the king was who had usurped the throne.

"My lord king," said the nurse, "for a twelvemonth after you went away all went well. Then, as no news of you came, men began to fall away from you. At last a foreign foe, called Shah Damak, learning of the state of the kingdom, came with a great army and battered down the gates of Magrur. He imprisoned the vizier, Nazarsaf, and seated himself on the throne. He is master of your treasures and your crown, and I know not how your will win them back."

When King Kamsen heard these bad tidings, he was as one distraught: taking a piece of paper, he wrote on it a challenge to Shah Damak, "Flee from my kingdom, dog, or come forth and fight."

The nurse carried Kamsen's challenge to Shah Damak, who asked where King Kamsen was and what troops he had with him. The nurse told him that Kamsen was alone, and that he was in the palace to the north of Magrur. Nevertheless Shah Damak, fearing a snare, collected a mighty army and led it towards the palace. When Kamrup saw the army advancing, she prayed to the fairies once more to help her. Instantly they came down from heaven, and, taking the form of giants, spread panic and death through Shah Damak's army. His soldiers scattered in all directions, but everywhere the fairies followed and slew them. Many surrendered to King Kamsen, and among those who surrendered was Shah Damak's young son, Shah Sadik: but Kamsen pitied his youth and spared him. Shah Damak was killed by the fairies as he fled.

After the fight was over, King Kamsen entered Magrur in triumph and freed the vizier Nazarsaf from the dungeon into which Shah Damak had flung him. Then, with Nazarsaf's help, he again mounted the throne of Sind. He built a great fort, to quell the disloyal, and ruled over Sind for many years afterwards with firmness, justice, and mercy. But of all his great possessions, he had no treasure that could compare with his beautiful queen, Kamrup, who had so often saved him, and with whom he had in the end returned safe and victorious to his kingdom and his people.

Dodo and Chanesar

Once upon a time there ruled in Rupa city a great prince, named Bhungar. He was of the Sumro clan and was king over all Sind. One day, as he went out a-hunting, he saw a lovely girl of the Lahar tribe sitting by his window. Although he saw her for only a moment, he could not get her beautiful face out of his thoughts. When he came back to his palace, he called his viziers and told them what had befallen, and vowed that he would wed the Lahar girl or die. The viziers laughed: "The king need not die," they said. "No Lahar girl would refuse the hand of a Sumro king." Then they went off and saw the girl's relatives: and, as they had promised the king, they soon arranged the marriage with her.

A year after their wedding, the Lahar girl bore her lord a son, to whom the king gave the name of Chanesar. Now King Bhungar had already a queen of the Sumro clan; and about the time Chanesar was born, this Sumro queen bore a daughter, to whom the king gave the name of Bhagi. A year late the Sumro queen gave birth to a son, whom the king called Dodo.

In course of time Dodo and Chanesar grew up: the king married Chanesar to a Lahar girl, and Dodo to a Sumro princess. Chanesar's wife bore him a son, Nangar, and Dodo's wife bore him a daughter, Kavel.

One day when Bhungar was with Chanesar's mother, she said sadly, "O! king, no words of mine can say how good you have been to me, or how happy you have made me. But when you die, the Sumro clansmen will drive me and Chanesar out of the palace and into the jungle." King Bhungar answered, "Nay, beloved, fear not: I will marry Nangar and Kavel, and then the Sumro clansmen will not dare to drive you out." That very day the king betrothed the little cousins to one another.

Some months later King Bhungar fell ill and died. Now the custom of Sind was that, until a successor had been chosen, the dead king could not be buried. In this way the throne of Sind was never empty. But when the men of Sind came to choose King Bhungar's successor, they could not agree. The Sumro clansmen said that Dodo was the true heir, as the son of a Sumro queen: but the other nobles said that Chanesar was the true heir, as he was born before Dodo. At last the vizier, Baran by name, said, "If a Sumro must succeed, then the true heir is Bhagi, the king's daughter, in that she was born before Dodo. Let her, therefore, give the throne, as she pleases, either to Dodo or to Chanesar." Even the Sumro clansmen agreed to this, for they felt sure that Bhagi would choose as heir her full brother, Dodo, rather than her half-brother, Chanesar. So the vizier Baran wrote to Bhagi, telling her that the throne was hers, and bidding her give it, as she pleased, either to Chanesar or Dodo. But Bhagi loved her elder brother the better, and she wrote back that she gave the throne to Chanesar. The Sumro clansmen bit their lips with rage; but, as they had agreed to ask Bhagi, they held their peace and sent for Chanesar.

When Chanesar saw the black looks of the Sumro nobles, his heart failed him and he said, "I must ask the queen, my mother. If she agrees, I will accept the throne." So Chanesar left the durbar, and went to his mother's chamber. There he fell at her feet, and said, "My mother, tell me, shall I take the throne in spite of the Sumros or shall I not?" His mother lifted up her son, and, putting her hand proudly on his shoulder, said, "Fear nothing, my son. Fortune is on your side. Take the throne and dare the Sumros."

But directly Chanesar had left the audience-room, the Sumro nobles burst into loud laughter and cried in scorn, "A fine king, forsooth! He cannot even wear a crown without asking his mother!" Then they called Dodo, and with drums and banners they took him through Rupa city and proclaimed him king. The noise of the procession reached the ears of Chanesar's mother and she sent a slave-girl to ask the cause of it. The slave-girl brought back the news that the Sumro nobles had rejected Chanesar, because he did not dare accept the throne without asking his mother. All the hopes of the Lahar queen died in her breast, and in her wrath she turned on Chanesar and said, "Yes, the Sumros are right; I bore, as I thought, a son, but I really bore a daughter. You, Chanesar, had better join the women at the loom and learn to weave." Chanesar's wife, too, no less angry at the loss of a crown, cried, "Nay, he is too stupid to learn to weave; let him fling a blanket over his shoulder and be a goatherd." Chanesar rose in a passion, and said, "A time will come when you will repent your words." So saying, he flung himself out of the women's rooms and sent word to Dodo: "The kingdom of Sind is mine. Give it back to me or I shall go to Delhi and ask the Emperor Alauddin for justice."

When Dodo got the message, his heart softened towards his brother; he called together his nobles, and, telling them Chanesar's words, said, "After all, he is my elder brother, and his son and my daughter are betrothed. Let him not go away in anger, but give him the kingdom. Then Sind will not be divided against itself and we two brothers will still be friends." But the Sumro nobles answered angrily, "Nay, O king, the kingdom is yours to rule, not to give in charity. If he asks for alms, give him some bullocks." King Dodo was silent, and Chanesar's message went back to him with the answer of the Sumro nobles. Instantly the prince turned his horse's head and rode towards Delhi.

As the young prince rode gloomily eastwards, he saw a goatherd sleeping in a meadow. At some distance the flocks were grazing and behind them the goatherd's staff was following of its own accord, heading off wanderers and driving in stragglers. By the goatherd's head lay his sword in a scabbard. Chanesar thought to himself that the man who had such a magic stick, must have a still more magic sword; and he began to steal softly towards the sleeping herdsman, that he might seize it. He had hardly walked two paces, when, to his horror, the sword rose upright from the ground and came hopping towards him. He cried aloud in terror, "Goatherd, gathered, catch your sword!" The herdsman got up and caught the sword: then turning to Chanesar, he said, "Fair youth you must have tried to steal either my stick or my sword; else the sword would not have attacked you." Chanesar confessed that he had tried to steal the sword, but he added, "Nevertheless, good goatherd, give me your sword, for I am in sore need of it." "Who are you?" asked the goatherd. "I am the son of King Bhungar, the Sumro," answered Chanesar proudly. "But which son—Chanesar or Dodo?" asked the goatherd; then he added, before the prince could reply, "But you must be 'Mammy Chanesar' (for that was the name the Sumros had given the prince), for Dodo is on the throne." "Yes," answered the prince humbly, "I am Mammy Chanesar: thus it is that I need your sword." "Very well," said the goatherd, "I will lend you my sword: but, when you return by this road, it will leave you and come back to me." He gave the sword to Chanesar, and the prince rode away with it to Delhi. As he neared the gate of the city, he saw a rakhshas sitting by the path, who forbade his entrance. At once Chanesar leapt from this horse, and with a single blow of his magic blade cut the rakhshas in two.

Thereafter Chanesar entered the city, and, going to the vizier, begged him to obtain for him an audience with the emperor. The vizier replied that the emperor would never see the prince in Delhi. "But," he added, "on a Friday, once every year, Alauddin holds a lion hunt. That Friday will soon be here. When the emperor is out hunting, I will present you to him." The prince rejoiced when he heard this, and resolved to win Alauddin's favour by his courage in the hunting-field.

When the day of the hunt dawned, the emperor went out to hunt a lion, attended by thousands of soldiers, for the beast's ferocity was known far and wide. Chanesar went to the vizier, and asked him whether the emperor was going to hunt one lion or an army of lions. "For in Sind," he said, "we always fight lions single-handed." The vizier gave no answer, but a few moments later he took Chanesar to the emperor and repeated his words. The emperor eyed the prince sternly, but the latter bore his gaze without flinching. Then the emperor said, "Chanesar shall make his words good. He shall show us here how they hunt lions in Sind. If he dies, the fault is his: if he kills the lion, great shall be his reward." The prince gladly assented.

When the cavalcade reached the lion's lair, Chanesar alighted from his horse, and, with the goatherd's sword in his hand, walked alone to meet the lion. As he drew near its lair, the furious beast rushed out and struck at him with its paw, but Chanesar jumped aside and cut the lion in two with his magic blade.

The emperor greeted the prince joyfully and begged him to name his reward. Chanesar told him his story—how he had been given the throne by his sister, and how the Sumro nobles had driven him out of Sind. "Protector of the world," he said, "the boon I ask is the throne of Sind." "You shall have it," said Alauddin, and he prepared a great army to conquer Sind for Chanesar.

The Afghan army set out for Sind, and when it passed the place where the goatherd lived, the magic sword, as the goatherd had foretold, left Chanesar, to his dismay, and returned to its owner. Nevertheless the prince rode on with Alauddin's army until it camped outside Dodo's city, Rupa.

When the Sumro nobles saw the vast host beyond their walls, fear entered their hearts; and they sent Chanesar's son, Nangar, as envoy to the emperor, bidding him say that if Alauddin went in peace, the Sumros would pay the cost of his army's going and coming, and would give the throne to Chanesar. The emperor, pleased with their submission, replied, "Put Chanesar on the throne, that is enough. Tell the Sumros that I remit them the cost of my army." But Chanesar wished to humble his enemies: so he said, "Nay, protector of the world, you must receive a gift from my hands in return for my throne. Take my sister Bhagi as your wife; then I shall know that our friendship will last always." "As you will," answered Alauddin kindly. Then turning to Nangar, he said, "Tell the Sumros that I shall marry the Princess Bhagi, so that our friendship may endure for ever."

But Nangar, although Chanesar's son, was no traitor like his father, and he answered Alauddin proudly, "No Sumro princess will ever wed a foreigner. If you wish to wed the Princess Bhagi,

you will have to win her first from our swords." Alauddin's face
grew black with anger at these words, and he bade his guards
seize Nangar. The boy prince fought gallantly, but at last fell,
covered with wounds. Chanesar put his dead body on a cot, and
sent it back to Rupa town. When the Princess Kavel, who had
been watching for her betrothed's return, saw Nangar lying dead
on the cot, she had a pyre prepared and burnt herself on the
young prince's body.

Inside the palace, Dodo's queen said to Bhagi, "Sister, why
should there be all this bloodshed for your sake? If your brother
would but give you to the emperor, the slaughter would cease."
So Bhagi rose and went to Dodo, and said, "Brother, why should
all this blood flow? Stay the fight and give me to Alauddin."

Dodo called together his Sumro clansmen, and put to them
the question, "Has a Sumro maiden ever been given in wedlock
save to a Sumro noble?" The Sumros replied, "We cannot say
for certain. But there is one Bhag, a mendicant, who knows
sixteen generations of Sumro kings; let him say."

King Dodo sent a palki for Bhag, had him brought to his
place, and bade him answer the question. "My lord king," replied
Bhag, "never during sixteen generations of Sumro kings has a
Sumro girl been given in wedlock save to a Sumro noble." "Then,"
said Dodo, "what my forebears would not do, I will not do. But
tell me of some spot where I may hide my wife and the wives
of the Sumro nobles." Bhag replied, "There is one Abro of Abrani
village: he will guard the Sumro women to the death." Then the
king bade Bhag go with a letter to this man.

Abro of Abrani greeted Bhag courteously, read the king's
letter, and bade Bhag tell Dodo that he would guard the Sumro
women to the death. Bhag gave Abro's message to the king; and,
at Dodo's bidding, he took the Sumro women to Abro of Abrani,

who welcomed them, and gave them his palace and all that he had. Then he sent word to Dodo, "Your queen and women are safe; now fight like a man, lest ruin befall Sind and the name of the Sumros die out of the land."

When Dodo learnt that his queen and sister and the other Sumro women were safe, he built trenches and glacis and pits, into which the emperor's horsemen might fall. Next he made himself a mighty weapon. Taking the handle of an oil-mill, he loaded it with lead: to one end he fastened four swords, and to the other three swords. Brandishing it fiercely, he led his men against the countless host of the Afghans.

At first the Sumro charge carried all before it; and Dodo, leading his troops, cut his way close to the emperor's throne. Alauddin asked Chanesar who the Sumro leader was. Chanesar answered, "That is my brother Dodo, who robbed me of my throne." "Though he robbed you of your throne," cried Alauddin, "he is the bravest of the brave." Dodo was about to shoot the emperor down with an arrow, but, hearing the Afghan's words, he lowered his bow.

"He is a noble foe," he said, "and I cannot kill him." Then Alauddin ordered his gunners to fire volleys at Dodo and his men; and beneath the hail of cannon-shot Dodo and the Sumros fell on the field. The emperor had search made for the king's body; and when it was found, he gave it to Chanesar. Chanesar, when he saw it, burst into tears. Alauddin, seeing the prince weeping, grew wroth. "You should have thought of this before you called me to Sind," he said sternly. "Had I known how brave Dodo was, and what a coward you are, I would never have helped you. Now go and bring me Bhagi and the Sumro women."

Chanesar went to Rupa, but it was quite empty. The men had fallen on the field: the women were with Abro of Abrani. Chanesar went back and told Alauddin, who wrote to Abro of Abrani, "Send me the Sumro women, and I will make you lord of Multan and Mathelo." But Abro sent back a haughty refusal, and made ready to fight the Afghan host.

At first Abro drove back the Afghan attacks, until none would lead them. Then Alauddin in person led his whole army to the assault. When Abro saw the mighty host, he went to Bhagi and the queen, and bade them have no fear. He would not leave them, he said, come what might; and he would draw, if need be, his last breath in their presence. Then taking with him his son, Mamat, and his remaining soldiers, he manned the walls against the Afghan charge. First Mamat fell, and Bhagi mourned him as a brother. Next Abro fell; but, remembering his promise to breathe his last in front of Bhagi and the queen, he had himself carried into the women's chambers to bid them good-bye. When the Sumro ladies saw that Abro lay a-dying, they prayed to God to shield their honour, as they had no other protector left. As the prayer left their lips, the kindly earth opened and swallowed them up.

The emperor stormed Abrani, and sent some sepoys into the women's chambers, to cut off Abro's head and bring it to him. The sepoys went; but so fierce was the dying man's look, that they feared him and fled back to Alauddin. The emperor rebuked them, and sent them again to fetch Abro's head: but this time Abro's little son, Dungarrai, who had been sleeping in his cot, awoke, and taking a toy sword in his hand, stood over his father to protect him. Again the sepoys returned to Alauddin, and told him about Dungarrai. "Send for him, protector of the world," they said: "he is so tiny that we have not the heart to kill him." Alauddin had Dungarrai brought to him; and then the sepoys went back once more, cut off Abro's head, and put it at the emperor's feet.

Alauddin was so pleased by the little boy's courage that he said, "I will make you, and not Chanesar, King of Sind." When he heard this, Chanesar cried in anger, "Am I to be flung aside after all my labours?" And calling on his friends, he fought the Afghan host so fiercely that, when he and his friends had fallen, the emperor had only seven of his horsemen left.

Alauddin crowned Dungarrai King of Sind, and took the road back to Delhi. But when he reached Mirpur Mathelo, he thought to himself: "I left Delhi with a countless host, how can I go back with but seven horsemen?" he halted at Mirpur Mathelo, and there had a tomb prepared. When it was ready, he took a poisoned pill, and, dying, was buried in the tomb. For this reason men call him to this day Alauddin Gori.[†] But the seven horsemen stayed by the tomb and their descendants may still be seen by its side as its "mujavars" or attendants.

[†] "Gori" is the Sindhi for pill. There is, of course, no truth in this story. Ala-ud-din's tribal name was Khilji, not Gori. He died at Delhi. His tomb may be seen there close to the Kutb Minar.